RISING TIDE

Emily Harrington returns to the Caribbean where she is reunited with old friends, romance ... and murder.

Emily Harrington returns to the stunning Caribbean island of Aruba for her friends' wedding, but finds herself plunged into danger again when the body of a beautiful young girl is washed up on the beach.

*Titles by Patricia Twomey Ryan
published by Severn House*

WINDSWEPT
RISING TIDE

RISING TIDE

Patricia Twomey Ryan

Severn House Large Print
London & New York

This first large print edition published 2015
in Great Britain and the USA by
SEVERN HOUSE PUBLISHERS LTD of
19 Cedar Road, Sutton, Surrey, England, SM2 5DA.
First world regular print edition published 2014
by Severn House Publishers Ltd.

British Library Cataloguing in Publication Data

Ryan, Patricia Twomey, 1946- author.
  Rising tide.
  1. Murder--Investigation--Fiction. 2. Weddings--Aruba--
  Fiction. 3. Romantic suspense novels. 4. Large type books.
  I. Title
  813.6-dc23

  ISBN-13: 9780727897961

Severn House Publishers support the Forest Stewardship
Council™ [FSC™], the leading international forest certification
organisation. All our titles that are printed on FSC certified paper
carry the FSC logo.

Printed and bound in Great Britain by
T J International, Padstow, Cornwall.

To John
With Love

PROLOGUE

The sun appeared – at first, a rosy glow on the dark horizon, but soon bright orange streaks followed by a sizzling yellow ball that seemed to burn the sky. Manchebo Beach was deserted this early in the morning and the white powder sand was unspoiled. The waves were gentler now, not steady and brisk as they were during the day, but still strong enough to carry discarded objects to the shore. A lone figure stood in the shadow of the Bucuti resort, watching silently as the waves rolled inward. The soft glow of a cigarette could be seen, but otherwise the world seemed empty.

The surf picked up and the waves quickened. An object, floating on top of the water, drifted in. Almost invisible, it took shape as it neared the shore – a body, long legs and arms outstretched, moving only to the rhythm of the waves. Long blonde hair streamed sinuously around the head that turned neither left nor right. With each incoming wave the figure grew closer until with one final push it was deposited on the sand. There it lay inert and still, oblivious to the brightening dawn.

The lone figure stared for a lingering moment. He knew it wouldn't be long before the body was discovered. With a slight shrug, he stamped out his final cigarette and walked away.

ONE

Emily stood facing her opened suitcase and started sorting through the neatly folded piles of clothes on her bed. She knew she had too much, but she was having the worst time making final choices. The navy-blue silk dress she had worn the last time she visited Island Bluffs hung on her closet door, but it was accompanied by soft aqua, lime green and bright coral dresses. Too many, she thought. She'd just take two, the navy and the aqua. Well, maybe the green also; it was, after all, a wedding. Perhaps the coral had been a mistake.

Taking a break, she headed into the kitchen, a galley like many New York apartments, and made a second cup of coffee. She was tired this morning. The last few days had been incredibly busy and she was looking forward to getting away.

The holiday had been lovely – Christmas Eve dinner at her father's big old house in

Croton with her sisters, Jane and Kate, their husbands and children in tow, and her brother, Brian, finally engaged to the very lively Rebecca. Her father had been in high spirits. Emily hadn't seen him so happy in years. After her mother's death from breast cancer ten years before, he had become quieter, more thoughtful and introspective. But this Christmas he'd seemed more like his old self, telling funny stories, playing with the grandkids and relishing the noise and laughter that filled the house. Emily had been taken aback when, after dinner, he broached the subject of selling the house. It was much too big, he said, and it was time he found a new place for himself. At first, Emily had tried to dissuade him.

'Dad, you've always loved this house and it's not that big. You have your office here, and all your books,' she reminded him.

But he had seemed pretty determined and her sisters and brother had been no help. 'It's time, Emily,' he had finally said with a rueful smile on his face. And in truth, Emily recognized that it was she who hated to think of the old house being sold. So many memories.

Checking her watch, Emily realized she had only an hour before the car arrived to take her to the airport. 'I better get moving,' she said out loud and, getting into vacation mode, she put on the Bob Marley CD she had bought at the airport last year.

It was small things like this that Emily most enjoyed about living alone. Michael would never have wanted to hear that music. Oh, it would be great to listen to if you were in the Caribbean but not back home, here in New York. Everything in its place. He would have rolled his eyes at her and she would probably have turned it off. But now she relished her freedom, and for just a moment she danced.

It had been a long year since she had been to the Bluffs. A long year and a lot of changes. She had known it was over with Michael when she left the Bluffs, but he had been stunned when she'd told him.

'Em, you've been through a terrible ordeal. You're upset, not thinking right.'

But she had been adamant. She knew that she would never really fit into his corporate law world, the white-shoe firm and his very conservative partners. And she knew Michael expected her to be the perfect partner's wife – maybe join the junior league or perhaps a book club, and the organizing committee for some *acceptable* charity. It was something she could never be. It wasn't the life for her.

They had discussed it endlessly those first few weeks. Michael had at first been apologetic: 'If I'd known what was happening, I would have come to the Bluffs no matter what. You know that, Em.' But she didn't know that. She thought of all the times over the last couple of years that Michael had not been there. Times she tried to ignore or make excuses for. And then he was angry. 'I don't know what you mean, Emily. The firm is so important for our future. Not just mine, both of ours. You knew what being a partner's wife involved. I thought you wanted that. That job of yours, those causes, I believed you'd give up all that.' And it was then she realized that Michael didn't know her very well at all.

After the anger came resignation. They'd put the apartment on the market and tried to be civil as they divided the furnishings. Emily noticed how few of the things Michael wanted. Not surprising, she realized, since most of the purchasing and decorating had been done by her. Michael never had the time. Now he had taken to saying they didn't really fit his 'lifestyle.'

Her new apartment was in the same building where she and Michael had had their two-bedroom place. It was smaller, and had no fireplace, but the bedroom was large enough to do double duty as her office, and when she awoke in the middle of the night, anxious about giving up the stability and safety of Michael, her computer was only a few feet away, calling to her.

She actually loved her new job – business, really – ECH Consulting, for Emily Claire Harrington, of course, and her early fears of not getting enough work had not materialized. She was able to use the skills and the contacts she had developed over the past six years with the state advocacy program, and she was always busy, sharing her talents and knowledge with foundations, human rights and environmental organizations – mostly NGOs, but even a few small government departments. She had always been an effective community organizer but now she was advising organizations on ways to be more effective responders. And she had done some traveling – San Francisco for the Carlton Foundation, Miami for the Dressler Group and Chicago for Bethechange.org.

Yes, she was content with her new life. She was beginning to find those pieces of herself she had left behind all those years before –

an enthusiasm for adventure, a willingness to take risks and a healthy sense of humor. The pieces she had left behind the summer she graduated from Cornell. The summer her mother had died.

Michael had moved to the Upper East Side, a bigger apartment in a modern building. Emily had seen it once when she'd had to drop off some signed papers to him. It was stunning, just what a young law firm partner would want.

Right, she thought, time for final choices. She knew there would be several formal events, the rehearsal tomorrow night and the wedding for starters, and certainly a beach barbecue. Dinner was always dressy at the Bluffs, so maybe the short silk print dress and her white linen trousers. Other than that, beach clothes and casuals would do. OK, these three, she thought, putting the long, softly flowing dresses carefully in her suitcase. Now for her jewelry. Her mother's sapphire earrings, definitely, to go with the dark blue; and gold – the hoop earrings, a couple of bracelets, and maybe the rose-gold necklace with the turquoise stone for the aqua dress. Done, she said, and then, without thinking, she slipped the gold bracelets into her pocket.

It wasn't long before the buzzer rang and Eddie was calling up to her. 'Your car is here, Miss Emily. Do you need help with your bags?'

'Not this time, Eddie,' she said, remembering last year's trip to the Bluffs – a freezing cold, snowy winter morning when she'd had to manage both her and Michael's bags. 'I'm traveling a lot lighter these days.'

The ride to the airport was uneventful. This January was milder than last year, and there were only traces of snow on the ground. Still, the rush to warmer climes was evident. When Emily got there, the airport was packed. But this time she headed for the first-class lounge, a benefit of her new business's success. She poured a cup of coffee and pulled out a book to read, but within a few minutes, her flight was being called.

It was easy settling into the wide leather seats with spacious overhead compartments and helpful cabin staff. Emily had the window seat. The older woman in the aisle seat just smiled as she sat down and soon took out a book. Emily was delighted; the quiet of the flight gave her time to think. In reality, she had had little quiet time in the last few months – certainly no time for a vacation – and although she loved every minute of what she was doing she knew it was time for some rest and relaxation.

She had been pleased when the invitation had arrived. She and the Maitlands, Annie and Martin, the owners of the Island Bluffs resort in Aruba, had stayed in touch since her visit the previous February. Not surprising really, that they had grown quite close during the course of what had been a sometimes difficult stay. They rarely revisited the circumstances surrounding Roger's death and, once the guilty plea had been entered and justice served, they all just wanted to leave it behind them. It had been months before references to the murder stopped appearing in every article about the resort: 'Island Bluffs, the beautiful Caribbean resort that was the site of last February's gruesome murder of travel critic Roger...' but eventually the press attention had died down.

Annie and Martin's daughter, Sarah, and her fiancé Jon Peterson had finally set the date for their wedding. Things had picked up for Jon since the trouble with Roger ended. His restaurant had been getting consistently great reviews and Annie said there was always a waiting list for reservations. The wedding was to take place at Island Bluffs on Saturday evening. Annie and Martin had closed the resort for the week, permitting wedding guests only – unprecedented, but they had warned all their regular guests early on, and a number of the regulars would even be at the wedding. Island Bluffs, as Emily had discovered the last time she was there, was much like a family, and Emily found herself looking forward to seeing them all again, especially one in particular...

TWO

'Fasten your seatbelts, ladies and gentlemen, as we prepare for landing.' The captain's voice alerted the passengers as the cabin crew bustled up and down the aisles, quickly collecting empty cups, old newspapers and plastic wrappers. Emily peered out the window for that beautiful first glimpse of the island and could easily make out the blue roof of Aruba's Reina Beatrix Airport. As she watched the white sand beaches and turquoise water come closer, the stewardess tapped the older woman sitting next to Emily, rousing her from sleep. 'The seatbelt light has come on, we're preparing for landing,' she said, and the woman quickly complied. Emily took a minute to reorganize her carry-on, putting in her iPad – her lifeline these days – her reading glasses and an unread magazine, and taking out her sunglasses and passport. As she walked through the airplane door the sun bathed her in its warmth and she quickly took off her blazer.

Even though Emily was in first class, the arrivals hall was crowded and there was already a line at customs. That was always the way with these winter flights. They arrived one after another and visitors often had to wait. Families struggled with carry-on bags, one being dragged by each of the adults, while each of the kids wheeled a rolling backpack. One father, with some impatience, trying to herd them on: 'Tommy, I told you to put the game away and the same goes for you, Sally – put your phone in your pocket until we get through customs.'

It took a while for the line to wind down, but Emily was not impatient. She believed she could have endured anything in this new-found warmth. And the three-piece steel band playing in the corner lifted everyone's spirits. Once through, Emily stopped to help a young woman, who looked close in age to her, with a baby. Emily saw she could not quite manage the car seat, diaper bag and documents she held in her hand. Emily was just reaching for the car seat when a young man, tall and with shaggy blond hair, brushed roughly by her, knocking her carry-on and blazer to the ground. She caught only a fleeting glimpse of him as she bent down to pick up her things.

'Really, watch where you're going,' the young woman exclaimed loudly. The young man turned, picked up Emily's blazer and threw it back to her, but walked quickly away, leaving her bag lying on the floor.

'Ugh, some people,' the young woman said, turning back to Emily. 'I'm so sorry. I just need to reorganize myself then I'll be fine. Thank you so much for the help.'

'Are you picking up a bag? I'm headed toward the baggage carousel – why don't we walk together?'

'Oh, that would be a big help. As soon as I can get her in the stroller I'll be all set. Thanks again.'

The baby's stroller came through right away and the young woman strapped her in and thanked Emily again.

'Sure you're all right?' Emily asked.

'We're fine now. I imagine our bag will come around soon.'

Emily found her own bag quickly, and as she walked towards the exit she saw Nelson, Martin and Annie's number two at the Bluffs, standing just beyond the door. 'Oh, Nelson,' she called, 'it's so good to be here.'

'*Bon bini*, Miss Emily,' Nelson said, reaching for her bag. 'It's good to see you again –

and on such a special occasion.'

'How is everyone, Nelson? They must all be so excited. Tell me about the wedding. What are the plans? Are Annie and Martin going to be able to relax and enjoy it? Are we picking up anyone else? Such a big undertaking and—'

'Whoa, Miss Emily. One thing at a time. First thing, into the car. Yes, we are waiting for one more guest. Ah, here she is now,' Nelson said as he hurried to help the young woman still struggling with baby in tow.

'Oh, how lovely,' Emily said as the woman and baby entered the car. 'I didn't realize ... you must be headed to Sarah's wedding also. I'm Emily – Emily Harrington.'

'Nice to meet you, Emily. I'm Peggy – Peggy Lawson – and this is my daughter, Maggie.' She stroked the side of the baby's face, triggering a toothy grin. Peggy's short, curly brown hair bounced as she leaned over to secure the baby in the car seat. She had dark, sparkling brown eyes and a quick smile – and she was petite, no more than five-two. At five-ten, Emily was aware of height. Growing up, she had always been the tallest girl in her class and had sometimes wished she could blend in with the others. Peggy looked across at Emily. 'Thanks so much for your help back there. I hope this trip wasn't a really bad idea, but I so wanted to be at Sarah's wedding and Ted, my husband, couldn't get the time off so I figured what the heck, how bad can it be?'

'I must say, I think you're brave making the trip on your own with a baby, but I'm sure the worst of it is over. Have you been to the Bluffs before?'

'Several times. Sarah and I became close friends years ago when she was in New York. It was before she met Jon. She hated everything else about the place. And she was so homesick. Once she and Jon got together things were better, but neither of them could imagine staying there. They couldn't wait to get back to Aruba. Anyway, I visit Sarah at the Bluffs when I can, and that's where Ted and I went on our honeymoon.'

'They do love the island and now that Jon's restaurant is doing so well...' Emily said, pausing as Maggie began to fuss. 'She must be exhausted, and you too!'

'She napped on the plane until we started to land and then ... It was the pressure on her ears, I suppose. Didn't you hear her?' Peggy said as she tried to soothe Maggie. 'Shush, shush, we're almost there.'

'I didn't,' Emily replied, not wanting to

offer that she had flown in first class. Somehow she couldn't quite get used to that. 'How old is she?'

'Nine months tomorrow. Sarah's her godmother.'

'She's precious,' Emily said, thinking to herself that it was just a year ago that she and Michael were contemplating a life that would soon include marriage and a baby. Sometimes she felt the loss of that life, but she knew it would never have worked out. She and Michael wanted different things – he security and safety; she, hmm ... what did she want? She still wasn't sure.

'Miss Annie told me to tell you not to worry about anything, Miss Peggy. She is all set for the baby,' Nelson said from the front seat. 'We are looking forward to it really. Not many babies at the Bluffs. You remember our lovely city of Oranjestad,' he continued, pointing out the gabled facades done up in a rainbow of colors: candytuft pink, buttercup yellow, bright tangerine and cool lime that lined the main streets. Emily loved the small, charming city with its profusion of plants, small shops and friendly people. Nelson waved and called to passers-by, and their lilting voices called back in greeting.

The ride from the airport was short and

Emily was glad they took the coastal road. She loved the view of the beaches with their white sand, blue water, colorful umbrellas and palapas.

'Now, just look how beautiful the day is,' Nelson offered. 'Here is Palm Beach, busy as always, and just ahead is Malmok. Not too much further now.'

Island Bluffs stood on the tip of the northern coast. The resort itself, situated on a hill, was shaped like a huge triangle. Jutting out from the land, it formed a narrow peninsula bordered on one side by a sheltered turquoise bay and on the other by the deep sapphire-blue ocean. The entrance was as stunning as Emily remembered. Beyond the stone pillars were cultivated lawns and gardens awash with deep emerald greens, vivid reds, startling yellows and intense purples. Emily could smell the sweet scent of the flowers – masses of hibiscus, bougainvillea and frangipani that lined walkways and entrances. The low buildings were white stucco and wood accented with the soft pastels and deeper hues that were the earmark of the Caribbean.

Annie waved from the front steps of the main house as the car pulled up. She looked lovely – tall and slim with flowing salt and pepper hair, a warm smile and bright green eyes. 'Emily, Peggy, how wonderful to see you both. And Maggie,' she said, reaching out for the baby. 'Oh, Peggy, she's just lovely. And how she's grown. Come, both of you. You must be hot and tired.'

The reception area was just as Emily remembered it – dark rattan furniture covered with white cushions and piled with pillows in vibrant hues, lush hanging plants and vases overflowing with dazzling cut flowers. Beyond, the four sets of open French doors created a seamless flow between the outside and the interior. As Emily and Peggy sat, Annie, with Maggie in her arms, could be heard calling out to Penny in Reception, 'Two rum punches, Penny, and please let Martin know that Emily and Peggy have arrived.

'Sarah's in town, Peggy. She'll be back in a couple of hours. You'll have just enough time to settle in before any of the craziness starts. Peggy is a bridesmaid,' Annie said, turning to Emily, 'along with Sarah's sister, Alex. Did you meet Alex last year, Emily? I can hardly remember.'

'No, Alex was in New York when I was here,' Emily answered, 'although, I heard a great deal about her.'

'Of course. One would think I'd remember everything about that week,' Annie's face clouded over for just a moment. 'Now, both of you are in suites that open directly onto the bay beach. It will be easier with the baby, Peggy, and the water is calm there. It's a short walk up the path to the main house, if you need anything, but I put you in the two suites at the end, so it'll be quieter.'

'That sounds perfect,' Peggy and Emily responded at the same time. Emily was happy to be on the bay beach side of the resort. She had loved the more rugged ocean beach last time and her rondoval had been beautiful but, after last year's horror, she didn't think she could be comfortable there.

'Emily,' Martin exclaimed, coming through the French doors. A good-looking man, with snow-white hair and a full mustache, he exuded energy and warmth. 'And Peggy, so good to see both of you. It's been much too long. And where is that beautiful baby? Ah, Annie, I should have known you'd have snatched her first thing. You've talked about nothing else all week. She's just beautiful, Peggy.'

Maggie started to squirm and soon whimper. 'Well,' Peggy said, taking her from Annie's arms. 'I recognize those sounds. It will

26

be a full roar shortly. Time for us to head to our room and hopefully have a nap. I know I'm ready for one.'

'Your bags are there already and there's some fruit and cheese and some snacks,' Annie said as Peggy strapped Maggie into the stroller. 'I've arranged for a mother's helper for the next couple of days. She's supposed to stop by later so you can meet her and she can get to know Maggie. Shall I say about four?'

'Perfect, thanks so much, Annie. Please let me know when Sarah gets back from town. I'm dying to see her. See you later, Emily and thanks again for your help.'

'I'll walk down with you, Peggy,' Martin said, stepping up to wheel the stroller. 'Don't go anywhere, Annie. There are a few details I need to go over with you.'

Emily watched as they headed down the path, and even from here she could hear Maggie's whimpers turn into giggles. 'What an adorable baby,' she exclaimed to Annie. 'And Peggy seems so comfortable and easy with her. Really relaxed. I don't know if I could be like that.'

'Oh, I'm sure you would. Peggy's the youngest of six and her older sisters and brothers all have big families. She's been around babies since she was one,' Annie laughed. 'And you've had your own experience raising kids.'

After Emily's mother had died, her father, overwhelmed with grief and loss, had buried himself in his work, and it was Emily who had taken over the major responsibility of raising her sisters and brother. She was determined that their big old Victorian house should remain as it always was, filled with life and laughter. A place where friends would feel comfortable hanging out, watching TV in the family room, talking for hours on the side porch or partying in the backyard.

'Oh, but those were not babies, Annie. Babies seem so helpless and fragile. Those were teenagers.'

'Believe me, I'd take babies any day! And they're not really so fragile – most of them are surprisingly resilient. But you're right – Peggy does seem to be wonderful with Maggie. She really is an amazing girl. She's been such a good friend to Sarah ... and Jon. Sarah had such a terrible time when she lived in New York. She was so homesick, not just for us, but for the island. It was Peggy who saw her through that. And then, of course, she met Jon. Right, I imagine you'd like to get settled. There's still time for a short swim and a nap before dinner. We're doing the rehearsal at seven and dinner right after, at eight.'

'Sounds great and I'm definitely heading to the beach for a bit. Everyone here looks so tanned and robust, and I feel so city pale. I can't wait to lie in that sun. And then take a nap.'

'I've seated you with the young crowd this evening, Emily. Sarah and Jon and Peggy and a few others, mostly their friends from the island and New York. And, of course, Thomas. I hope that's all right?' Annie asked with a questioning glance.

Emily could tell from her look that she wanted to ask more but didn't want to be intrusive. Emily was unsure of what to say.

'That's perfect, Annie,' was the best she could do, trying to hide her smile as she headed down the path.

THREE

The bay beach was lively as Emily made her way to her suite. Music with a soft Caribbean beat serenaded those swaying in the rope hammocks and stretched out on wooden lounge chairs laid out with thick blue cushions. There was the lively sound of chatting and laughter, old friends sharing stories and catching up, conversations similar to those that Emily remembered from her last visit. The further she walked from the beach bar, the quieter it got. And as she passed what she thought was Peggy's suite, she heard the sweet strains of a lullaby through the window.

Emily's suite was just what she imagined it would be: pure white walls, dark wooden floors and a four-poster bed draped with the softest of netting and dressed in crisp white linens. Splashes of color – vibrant red, emerald green and deep magenta – popped out from the throw pillows and local wall art. A white upholstered chaise longue sat in front of the shuttered window and on a nearby table sat an ice bucket with a split of champagne, a small cheeseboard and a bowl of fresh fruit. As soon as she saw this, Emily realized that she was starving.

She loved the atmosphere at Island Bluffs. Martin and Annie Maitland, who'd founded the resort over thirty years ago, had a reputation for knowing each guest by name and prided themselves on the sense of family the place maintained. This club-like mood soon spread among their guests, many of whom made fast and long-lasting friendships. They would return the same time each year looking forward to seeing each other again. The resort was visually stunning, meticulously maintained and incredibly safe. There were no locks on the doors, the staff was well paid and respectfully treated, and Martin and Annie were active participants in not just the resort life of Aruba but their local community.

The suite was cool, the blistering afternoon sun blocked by the shutters and the air swirling lightly to the rhythm of the ceiling fan. Emily took off her jeans, designer for this trip, and her damp T-shirt and let the fan's breeze cool her heat-drenched body.

Stretching out on the chaise, she poured a small glass of champagne, nibbled on the cheese and fruit and allowed her mind to wander.

Thomas was her first thought. Hmmm, how long had it been since she had seen him? Almost ten months. Thomas Moller was the chief inspector who had handled the murder investigation after Roger Stirhew's body had been discovered on the beach by Emily. He was tall, tanned and handsome with a quiet, steady manner, a shy smile, piercing blue eyes and an unruly crooked parting to his sandy hair. Her first impressions of him had been colored by the investigation – serious, determined, logical – the type of person who would inspire respect but perhaps not affection. Yet, as the investigation went on, this serious side was tempered by warmth, and once it ended Emily saw the full picture of Thomas.

She thought now about those few days that they had spent together last year after Roger's killer had been caught. What great fun they had had doing all of the things that a first-time visitor would do. Emily was sure they were things that he had done many times, but his enthusiasm never wavered.

That first morning Thomas had arrived at

the Bluffs in an open green Land Rover, with a packed cooler and a map, and proceeded to give Emily the grand tour. They'd started out at Arikok National Park, home to many native species like the Aruban parakeet and the Aruban burrowing owl. Emily had not been so charmed by the Aruban rattlesnake, but the herds of donkeys and goats were adorable. They'd spent all morning hiking the trails and seeing the unusual land formations made from lava, quartz and limestone. Thomas hadn't known whether Emily would want to visit the caves in the park, but she'd been anxious to. She'd heard about the primitive drawings on the walls, and entering Huliba Cave with Thomas was nothing like the bat cave experience she had had previously. She'd been touched to see Thomas blush as he explained the caves nickname, 'Tunnel of Love', due to its heart-shaped entrance, and as they'd bent to enter the darkened inside, Emily had felt reassured by his arm that gently circled her shoulders.

It had been after noon by the time they'd left there and headed to a beach along the windward coast, where they'd picnicked beside one of the inlets formed over time by the ocean's pounding waves. Thomas had been full of information about the island and had entertained Emily all afternoon with charming stories of the place and the people. Emily had found herself convulsing with laughter as Thomas, an incredible mimic, did impressions of some of the more colorful people at the Bluffs. And he hadn't spared himself, either. Emily had loved this side of him, filled with humor and enjoyment. It had been late afternoon when they'd returned to the Bluffs. Thomas had had to work that evening but Emily agreed to spend the next day continuing their exploration. Just as he was leaving, he'd turned, almost as an afterthought, and kissed Emily lightly on the lips.

Over the next two days they had enjoyed all the island had to offer. They'd crossed the Natural Bridge, a formation of coral limestone cut out by years of ocean surf that is one of the largest natural spans in the world. On the northern coast, they'd explored an abandoned gold mill that processed ore during Aruba's nineteenth-century gold rush. They'd visited the California Lighthouse, the stone lighthouse named after the S.S. *California*, a wooden sailing ship that had sunk near shore, and then walked to the nearby white sand dunes to watch the kids go dune surfing. Emily had been both intrigued and amused when Thomas actually took a turn sliding down the steep dune.

They'd swum and snorkeled and sailed. And at night they'd gone to elegant restaurants and local hot spots. They'd drunk Azul Caribes under a giant palapa at Moomba Beach, and taken an Aruba salsa lesson at Mambo Jambos. They'd listened to a calypso band at the popular Senor Frog bar on Palm Beach, and taken a turn dancing to fiery tumba at Mr Jazz. On Emily's last night they had walked along the ocean beach, counting a million stars.

Clearly their friendship had been evolving, becoming something different, something much closer to romance, but they'd both known that it was too soon for Emily to go down that route. Even though her relationship with Michael was over, she still had to return to New York, where there were unresolved problems and complications yet to work out.

She and Thomas had stayed in touch once she'd returned home, and he had been a source of comfort during the difficult days with Michael. He had been willing to listen endlessly – supportive as she questioned what she was doing, reassuring as she berated herself for hurting Michael, encouraging as she moved forward with her decision and started to make the changes in her life. Sometimes, after a particularly difficult day, she'd curl up in bed and talk to him for hours. And as the issues with Michael – the break-up, the apartment, telling their families and friends, many mutual by now – began to be resolved, Emily had found herself yearning to see Thomas again. The wedding provided the perfect opportunity but, now that it was here, Emily found herself anxious.

Well, lying here daydreaming will get me nowhere, she thought, getting up and quickly unpacking her suitcase. She hung the dresses carefully, checking for wrinkles. Not bad, but she would steam them quickly in the bathroom before she wore them. She would wear the lime green one for the rehearsal dinner tonight. She placed her make-up bag in the bathroom, hung her blazer in the closet and put her jewelry in the box on the dresser. Once finished, she put on her bathing suit, grabbed her tote bag and headed for the beach.

The late afternoon sun was glorious, not as hot as midday but bright and sparkly on the water. The beach was almost empty, as it usually was at this time. There was a slight breeze and Emily chose a lounge chair under a palm. She dropped her stuff and headed to the water's edge. She never could get over how clear it was, watching as her toes sank deeper and deeper. A couple of small fish, one blue with silver stripes and one with a yellow tail, swam by and Emily dove right in. The water was refreshing, not too cold like the ocean could be, and Emily swam back and forth, stretching her tired muscles. Then she turned on her back and just floated on the surface of the water, quieting both her body and her mind.

As she emerged from the water and headed back to her chair, she espied a familiar figure walking down the path towards the beach. Thomas. His suit jacket slung over his shoulder, tie loosened, hand screening the sun from his eyes. Her heartbeat quickened and she was suddenly unsure. He saw her immediately, calling out her name as he hastened his step.

'Emily,' he said as he reached her, grasping her shoulders and pulling her towards him. 'Emily, it's so good to see you.'

'Oh, Thomas, I ... I'm ... it's...' Emily stumbled over her words, overwhelmed suddenly by his presence. 'It's been so long and I've been so wanting—'

'I can't stay, Emily. I have a couple of things to finish up at work but I had to see you, even just for a minute. I'll be back later. The rehearsal's at seven and I'll see you right afterwards. And Emily, I have the next five days off. Plenty of time for us to catch up, hang out, go sailing. We have to go sailing. I can't wait.'

Emily could barely get a word in, but she didn't need to. It was clear from Thomas's words what his feelings were and as he spoke Emily's feelings also became clearer. Five days together. Time. Time to talk and laugh. Time to explore the island and explore each other. Perhaps time enough to figure things out.

'I better go or I'll never get back by seven,' Thomas said, and with a quick kiss on the cheek he was gone.

Emily smiled as she returned to her lounge chair and looked around her. Had the water ever been this blue, the sky this bright, the flowers this vibrant? She closed her eyes and let her hand drift to the sand. Had the sun ever been this warm, the sand this soft, the breeze this gentle? The warmth of Thomas spread through her and she soon drifted off to sleep.

But it was short-lived as she heard talking

and laughter behind her. 'Peggy, here, let me help,' she called out, seeing Peggy struggling carrying Maggie, a bag and a rolled mat across the sand.

'Thanks, Emily,' Peggy said, dropping her stuff on the lounge chair next to Emily. 'Seems like this is your job every time you see me. I'll try not to let it happen too often.'

'No problem.' Emily reached for Maggie. 'Here, let me hold her while you set up.'

Peggy unrolled the brightly colored mat on the sand. 'This was in my room,' she said. 'Annie must have left it there. And a basket filled with everything a baby could need or want – extra diapers, a sun hat, sunscreen – seventy-five SPF. I don't think I've ever seen seventy-five before. This pail and shovel, some water toys.'

She put the pail and shovel, a sippy cup with water, a shape-sorter box and two small board books on the mat and reached for Maggie. 'The mother's helper should be here any minute.' She sat Maggie down and flopped onto the lounge chair. 'I'm still exhausted. I'm afraid it was a short nap and by the time I unpacked Maggie was awake, but hopefully it will mean an early bedtime.' She paused and glanced at Emily. 'I don't mean to pry, but Sarah mentioned that there might be a romance brewing for—'

'Peggy,' they heard Annie call from the path before Emily had a chance to say anything. Walking with her was a beautiful young girl, thin and tall with long legs, blonde hair that reached well below her shoulders and the deep blue eyes that were so prevalent in Aruba. 'Peggy, let me introduce Ariana Van Meeterens,' Annie said, turning towards the young girl. Emily imagined her to be about seventeen.

'Hi, Ariana.' Peggy reached out her hand as Ariana gave a soft hello.

'And this is Maggie.' She gestured towards the baby, who had turned her head up to see who was there and smiled a perfect smile.

'Oh, she's so cute. How old is she?' Ariana asked.

'Just turned nine months, and yes, she is cute but don't be fooled – she can be a handful.' And as if to demonstrate that, Maggie picked up her pail of sand and dumped it over her head. Peggy bent to rescue her from the cascading sand and Ariana joined her on the mat.

'Ariana is on her winter break so she'll be able to help out for several days,' Annie explained. 'She has lots of experience with little kids. She's one of the most sought-after babysitters on the island. She'll be greatly missed when she goes off to college in the fall.' Ariana blushed.

Emily noticed how quickly Ariana was able to engage Maggie. She started filling up the bucket with sand again, but when Maggie pushed it away (perhaps remembering what had just happened), she quickly picked up one of the board books. *'Mama duck had five little ducklings,'* she began, making quacking noises as she read. Maggie giggled with each quack.

'Oh, that's great,' Peggy said, slowly getting up from the mat to let Ariana and Maggie play together.

'She can stay for about an hour now and then come back this evening and mind her during the rehearsal and dinner. Till about ten, I think. Is that right, Ariana?'

'Ten is fine, even eleven is OK.' Ariana seemed easy-going and perceptive, sensing quickly when Maggie was losing interest in what they were doing. 'Can I take her down to play in the water?' she asked. 'She seems to be getting bored playing here.' She stood up and took off her Dance Aruba T-shirt.

'Oh, what's happened to your arm?' Annie said, reaching out to stroke the fiery bruise on Ariana's right arm.

'Oh, that,' Ariana answered, and looked away for a moment. 'It's nothing. I'm just so clumsy.' She shrugged. 'We'll just play at the edge and then maybe I could take her for a walk in the stroller.' She looked at Peggy as she slipped the T-shirt back over her head.

'Be my guest,' Peggy said. 'I'd love to take a short snooze here on the beach.'

'OK then,' Annie answered. 'I'll leave you all to it. Time for me to head up to the house and see how all the rehearsal arrangements are coming along.'

'I think I'll head back to my room. A nap before dinner sounds like a great idea,' Emily said, but Peggy already had her eyes closed.

FOUR

Emily woke from her nap energized and
excited. She opened the shutters and looked
out at the darkening sky. Night had fallen
while she was napping and she knew she
needed to hurry now. The rehearsal must be
underway and that meant under an hour till
dinner, but she could not resist stepping outside to see the moon's ascent. Bright twinkling stars began to appear and she could hear
the soft lapping of the water. The air was
cooler than this afternoon but pleasant, with
the same soft breeze. As she sat for a moment she heard a sound on the path that led
to the main house. In the distance she saw
what looked like three figures, a man, a
woman and a child in a stroller. She realized
that it must be Ariana with Maggie, but as
she looked the third figure seemed to dis-
appear; maybe it had never been there.

As they got closer, Emily raised her arm to
wave and Ariana noticed her.

'Whoa,' she said, her voice surprised. 'I didn't see you there.'

'Sorry, I didn't mean to startle you. Looks like Maggie wasn't ready to fall asleep.'

'Not by a long shot. She was a little upset when Peggy left so I put her in the stroller and walked up to the rehearsal. She was much happier outside so I thought we should just keep walking around. I'm hoping she gets sleepy.'

'Well, she looks pretty sleepy now,' Emily said, seeing Maggie's drooping eyes. 'Has the rehearsal started?'

'Just a few minutes ago. On the beach in front of the main house. It seems to be going pretty well. Sarah will be a beautiful bride. She's so lucky.'

'I'd better get ready,' Emily said, opening the door to her suite. 'Good luck; I hope she settles down.'

Emily hung her lime-green dress in the bathroom and ran the hot water for several minutes until the steam took care of the last of the wrinkles. She took out her strappy green sandals, with heels, and placed them by the bed. They had been an unusual purchase for her. Michael, only an inch taller than Emily, had never liked her wearing high heels. She showered and dressed quickly, leaving her red hair loose around her shoulders, anxious now to get to the main house. Dinner, she knew, would be an elaborate affair held at the resort's restaurant, Pepperhearts.

The moon had risen higher in the sky and it cast a silvery glow on the water and the sand. As she walked along the path, she savored the sweet smell of the bougainvillea. Up ahead, she could see the twinkling white lights that draped the small trees at the entrance to the restaurant. It was a beautiful space, open to the night with a series of terraces leading all the way down to the sea wall. She could see many of the guests were already sharing cocktails, and their conversation and gentle laughter filled the night.

'Emily,' a voice called as soon as she entered. 'My dear, we're over here.' I'd recognize that voice anywhere, Emily thought with a laugh. And there before her was a tall, perfectly coifed woman, her patrician face meticulously made up, highlighted with smoky eyeshadow and luminescent lips. Her incredibly thin frame was draped tonight in a deep emerald gown with a rhinestone-trimmed halter top that emphasized her long, thin neck.

'Marietta, it's wonderful to see you,' Emily

said as she joined her on the terrace. Marietta St. John was an aging New York society columnist. The only daughter of the black sheep of a prominent family, she had used her name and connections to make a career for herself. A frequent guest at the Bluffs, she had been caught up in last year's murder of Roger Stirhew, and had even been a suspect for a brief time.

'You look just lovely, my dear. Now, I hope you are heeding the advice I gave you last year. Not too much sun. I see you've already gotten some today. You're so fair. It will only bring out more freckles. Isn't this a marvelous occasion? I couldn't be happier for Sarah and Jon, especially after all that nastiness last year. And, of course, for Annie and Martin, too. And tell me, my dear, what *is* happening with you and that...'

Emily was spared from answering Marietta's question by the arrival of Nora, Marietta's constant companion. 'Oh, Nora, look who's here. It's *our* Emily, and doesn't she look wonderful?'

A pleasant-looking woman in her late fifties, Nora Richards had undergone a remarkable change since Emily had seen her last. She was no longer chubby and plain looking, trying desperately to blend into the background. Tonight she was stylishly dressed and self-possessed, comfortable as she came to Marietta's side.

'Hello, Emily, it's so good to see you again and yes, Marietta, she does look lovely. Now, here are your pills and you really must try to remember them.'

'I know, I know. I *do* try, dear, really, I do,' Marietta answered, placing her hand gently on Nora's arm. 'You've heard our news, Emily?'

Emily certainly had heard their news. Although she had become quietly aware of it during last year's investigation, it had created quite a stir when Marietta St. John had come out, revealing to the world that her long-time companion was in fact her partner.

'Of course, I always believed you suspected last year, and Nora and I so wanted to tell you, but we just weren't ready. After we returned to New York, we talked and talked about it and decided that it was time to tell the truth and we would deal with the consequences. And, well, you know, my dear, simply everyone is doing it.'

Emily laughed as she answered. 'I did hear, Marietta, and you created quite a stir in New York.'

'Oh, *not* just in New York, my dear, no, no. *Everywhere*. You cannot imagine the letters I received, so...'

Just then everyone's attention turned to the terrace steps as the wedding party entered the dining room. Sarah practically glowed as she held Jon's hand and waved to the guests. Alex and Peggy followed behind, and Thomas and a friend of Jon's from New York followed them.

Martin, always the consummate host, walked to the center of the room. 'I just wanted to take this moment to welcome all of you,' he said with a sweep of his arm. 'This is a very special occasion for us, one we've been anticipating for some time, and Annie and I thank you for sharing it with us. It seems like only yesterday that our lovely Sarah was—'

'Oh, no, you don't,' Annie said, laughing as she joined Martin in the center of the room. 'Save your speech for tomorrow. I think the father of the bride is only allowed one. But let me repeat Martin's words – your presence makes this occasion all the more special for us. And now, a glass of champagne for all.'

With that cue, waiters filed onto the terraces carrying trays filled with sparkling glasses. The small steel band struck a mellow Caribbean tune and everyone started to mingle. Thomas immediately made his way over to Emily. 'Emily, you look lovely,' he said, giving her a quick hug. Then, turning: 'Marietta, Nora, it's good to see you again, and in much happier circumstances.'

'Inspector,' Marietta said, holding out her hand.

'No, no. No inspector tonight. Thomas, please.'

'Of course, Thomas,' she replied. 'It is a wonderful occasion. I simply love weddings, don't *you*, Emily?'

Emily and Thomas quickly escaped the inquiring eyes of Marietta and headed over to where Sarah and Jon were standing with friends.

'Sarah, it's wonderful to see you. Thank you so much for inviting me,' Emily said.

'Oh, Emily, after all you did for Jon ... I shudder to think of what might have happened if you hadn't ... And anyway, our best man practically insisted.'

'There was no practically about it,' Jon added as Thomas actually blushed.

'Enough, enough,' Thomas said, laughing. 'Any more of this and Emily and I are going to sit by ourselves for dinner.'

Dinner was delightful but decidedly low

key. It was clear that Annie and Martin wanted the evening to be relaxing and finish early; after all, they had a very big day tomorrow. Emily and Thomas enjoyed being part of the 'young crowd' as Annie had put it. There was much laughter as the group shared stories and jokes. As many of them were to do with New York City, Emily felt a part of the conversation right away, but Thomas was a bit quiet. He was the only one who had never been to New York and gave up trying to play catch-up with the group. And although they enjoyed the dinner, he and Emily were anxious to spend some time alone.

FIVE

It was close to ten when the dinner ended. Most of the guests headed back to their rooms or to their homes if they were islanders, and cheerful goodnights filled the air. Jon and Sarah were headed back to Oranjestad, and Peggy was anxious to see how Maggie had fared. Emily and Thomas spent a few minutes talking to Annie and Martin, who seemed delighted with the evening and for once didn't stay around for the clean-up. They had brought in plenty of extra staff, hoping to enjoy these few days. The night was beautiful and surprisingly quiet by the time they left the main house, so Emily and Thomas decided to take a walk on the beach.

They had only gone a short distance along the softly lit path when a figure approached from the bay beach. Emily strained to see who it was but it was difficult to see beyond the path. It wasn't until they were quite close that she realized it was Ariana.

'Oh, it's you, Ariana. Sorry, it's so hard to see beyond the lights. How did the evening go?'

'It was great. Maggie is adorable and after we walked for a while she settled down. And as soon as we got back to the suite she went to sleep. I wish all the kids I minded were that easy. Well, guess I'll see you tomorrow. I'm coming back before the wedding so Peggy can get ready. 'Bye.'

'Goodnight,' Emily said, watching Ariana walk towards the resort exit. And then, noticing how deserted it seemed, she call-ed out, 'Wait, Ariana, how are you getting home?'

'Oh, don't worry about me,' she called back over her shoulder and pointed to a car idling beyond the front gate. 'A friend is picking me up. See you.'

'Such a sweet girl,' Emily said to Thomas as they walked along. 'She's helping mind Peggy's baby over the next couple of days. Her parents are good friends of Annie and Martin. Annie thinks of everything ... You seemed kind of quiet tonight.'

'Did I? Yeah, I guess I did. It's funny – seeing Jon and Sarah getting married makes me feel ... sad, somehow. Oh, not for them, it's great for them, but it just makes me wonder what I'm doing with my life. Jon has done so much: moving to New York, becoming a chef – something that he loves, even though his parents weren't too happy – the restaurant, and now this. I don't know.'

'I thought you loved what you're doing, Thomas.'

'I do, but ... You know, when I was young I wanted to be a teacher or a writer. I wanted to study history and literature and classics. I loved school. More than anything I wanted to go to college, but there wasn't much chance of that.'

Emily remained quiet, wanting to give Thomas the time he needed.

'You see, my father drank. Not so much when I was real young, but more and more. By the time I got to high school he had no job and his health was broken. My mother wasn't able to stop him. He was never mean or angry really, just depressed and sad. Whatever his demons were, I never found out.'

Thomas went on to talk for a long time. It seemed that once this door opened he could not close it until he had said it all: his father's death, his mother's illness, leaving school and eventually joining the police force. Seemingly coming to terms with it all, but now ... well, perhaps not.

It was after midnight as they headed towards Emily's suite. 'Sorry, Em, I imagine that was more than you bargained for?'

Emily turned towards him, looked into his eyes and gently stroked his cheek. 'Don't ever say that, Thomas. I can never repay you for all the nights you listened to me, never becoming tired of my uncertainty, always reassuring. It's all part of...' And with that, Thomas drew her to him and kissed her. Emily was drawn by the intensity of his lips and the gentle pressure of his hand on her lower back urging her closer. For a moment she felt herself melt into him.

She hated for the evening to end, but she knew that Thomas was emotionally drained. 'We should call it a night,' she said. 'You have a busy day tomorrow.'

'I know, you're right, but let's spend the morning together,' Thomas said, his mood brightening. 'Let's go sailing. I'd love for you to see *Tranquility*; she's a beauty. If we get out early we can be back by noon. I don't really have anything to do till late afternoon. Let's, Emily.'

SIX

Emily rose early, showered and dressed quickly, put her hair up in a ponytail, grabbed a baseball cap and her tote bag and headed out the door. It was a beautiful morning, with a brilliant sun and a light breeze. Perfect for sailing. Few people were awake this early at the Bluffs, but on the path she met Peggy wheeling Maggie.

'I know why I'm up at this ungodly hour, but what are you doing up? Hope we didn't wake you.'

'No, no. I didn't hear you guys at all. Thomas and I are going sailing. Just for a couple of hours, but we have to get an early start.'

'So what's the story with you two? Like I said, Sarah mentioned something. He seems nice, a little quiet, and damn, he's good looking.'

'No story yet, but we'll see.'

She and Peggy had a quick breakfast at the beach bar, the only place to eat since the restaurant was being prepared for the wedding reception. Annie joined them for a few minutes.

'You two, or three, I should say, are up early. How did Maggie sleep, Peggy? And how did Ariana work out?'

'Maggie slept great. She's a good sleeper, but an early riser. And Ariana was a godsend. She's obviously good with kids. But you must be exhausted, Annie.'

'A little tired, but last night worked out so well. Everything went smoothly and I think everyone enjoyed themselves and it ended early! Just as we planned. You're up awfully early, Emily.'

'Thomas and I are going sailing,' Emily said, and couldn't help the wide smile that crept across her face.

'How wonderful. Perfect morning for it,' Annie said with a smile just as wide. 'Don't forget Marietta's advice, "not too much sun" or you'll never hear the end of it. Now I better get back to the restaurant. We have a ton of things to do. Ah, there's Thomas now.'

Thomas stood at the top of the path near the main house and waved. Peggy's right, he is damn good looking, Emily thought as she hurried toward him.

It took only a short time to reach the

Varadero Marina where Thomas had docked his boat, and Emily could sense his pride as he showed it to her. 'It's an old boat, a 1977, called a Bristol Channel Cutter,' he told her. 'It was a real mess when I bought it. I did most of the restoration myself. Actually took me a couple of years.'

'It's beautiful, Thomas,' Emily said, taking in the dark blue hull, teak deck and tall mast, everything gleaming in the morning sun. 'How big is it?'

'Twenty-eight feet. The cabin's got a galley, a head and a small salon. It's amazing what fits in there – a table and benches that unfold into a bed. I've taken her out for a week at a time. Sailed islands east and west. Now, it's time for us to get to work.'

The morning flew by as Emily and Thomas sailed the bay waters. They relished the warm sun, billowing clouds and brisk morning breezes that filled the sails. Emily was a quick learner, doing everything from securing the lines to unfurling the sail. And Thomas was a patient teacher. She was amazed at his skill and strength as his muscles strained to turn the stern into the wind.

'Maybe after the wedding we could go out for the whole day. Try the ocean. It's tricky but exhilarating,' Thomas said as they headed back into shore.

'I'd love that, Thomas.'

It was late by the time Emily got back to the Bluffs, and the wedding preparation seemed to be in full swing. A bamboo arbor dressed in white netting and flowers stood on the beach with white wooden chairs positioned in rows before it. The restaurant dining room was abuzz with workers, setting tables, arranging flowers and polishing silver, and Annie and Martin were right in the middle, directing everything.

Emily grabbed something quick to eat and headed for the beach. It was busy and she was glad to find a lounge chair over where Peggy and Maggie were sitting in the shade of a palm.

'How was the sail?' Peggy asked.

'Glorious,' Emily answered. 'I've never sailed before and I loved it.'

'And the story?'

'Hmmm? Oh, that story. I think it's coming along. Coming along nicely. How was your morning?'

'Good, but busy. Mostly spent trying to keep Maggie entertained. She actually took an early nap right here on the beach.'

'You must be exhausted. Why don't I keep an eye on Maggie and you go get some rest.

You have a long night ahead of you and I can nap later.'

'Really, you're a saint, Emily. If I can just get forty-five minutes that would do it.'

Emily spent the next hour with Maggie. They played in the sand and sat at the water's edge. Maggie splashed in puddles and picked up tiny handfuls of wet sand that invariably ended up all over her. Then Emily would pick her up and slowly wade into the bay, letting the warm water wash over them. Maggie thought this was great fun and they did it five or six times before she got bored. Emily was just about to take her for a walk when Peggy emerged from her suite.

'My God, I'm a new woman,' she said with a laugh. 'I owe you big time. How was she?'

'Great, easy as anything,' Emily answered, realizing that it was true. 'Well, time for me to head to my suite. What time is Ariana coming?'

''Bout five-thirty, I think. I'm getting dressed up at the main house and we're doing pictures and stuff. I hope Maggie will be OK. It'll be a long night for Ariana.'

Emily headed to her suite. As always, a snack plate and split of wine waited for her. Before napping she took a few minutes to relive her morning with Thomas. The sail had been great, but even more engaging had been Thomas's company. Seeing him like that, so carefree out on the water, so open and animated ... It was another side of him that drew her to him even more. The night promised to be special in so many ways.

Emily showered and dressed, choosing to wear the same navy silk dress she had worn last year at the Bluffs. She loved the light, soft fabric that skimmed her body as it floated softly to the floor. It was perfectly simple, the only adornment a beaded clasp at the single shoulder, and she accessorized it with just her mother's sapphire-blue earrings, their deep color bringing out the blue of her eyes. For a moment she looked at herself in the mirror – her red hair drawn back and piled softly at her crown, her pale skin with its light freckles and soft blush from the sun, her tall, thin body almost shimmering as she moved. She was content with what she saw.

When she arrived at the bay beach she paused at the beauty of the setting. The sun was just beginning its slow descent and the sky was marbled with gold, lavender and pink streaks. A white runner ran the length of the sand and urns with tall green sea grass stood at the end of each row. Most of the guests had arrived, mingling and greeting each other. Emily was pleased to see Jessica, Roger Stirhew's wife. Roger had both saved and almost destroyed Jessica, although he wasn't the only one.

'Jessica, it's so good to see you. How are you?' Emily said, noting how good Jessica looked, rested and relaxed. Her hair was cut short and her eyes had lost that haunted look. She wore a simple patterned silk dress with peach slides. She looked ... how to describe it? She looked comfortable.

'Emily, you look wonderful. Good to see you too. It's hard to imagine that the last time ... I couldn't miss the wedding but I couldn't stay here at the Bluffs. Annie made arrangements for me to stay in town, at a lovely guest house, quiet and secluded.'

'That sounds perfect. How has life been treating you?' Emily asked, not sure whether Jessica wanted to share news of what must have been a very difficult time.

'It's been OK. It was hell at first, for me and even more so for Jason.'

Emily could imagine how difficult things were for Jason. In spite of everything, Roger had been Jason's father, after all. 'But I think we're doing all right now. We've moved, you know. That house was too big and held too many memories. My mother is with us now.

It's been good for her ... and for us. What happened with—'

'Michael? That's over. It was over the day I left the Bluffs. It's been a year of incredible changes, but I have to say I think I'm doing OK too. Did Jason come with you?'

'No, he's at home with my mom. I won't be staying long, but I so wanted to see Sarah and Jon. And Annie and Martin, of course. They've been so kind over the past months, always keeping in touch. There at my side during the trial; Martin visiting when he's in the States. It's meant a lot.'

At that moment a string quartet started playing and the guests began to take their seats. Emily and Jessica sat together just behind Marietta and Nora. Emily recognized a number of the other guests: the psychiatrist and his wife, the doctor whose daughter, or was it son, was looking for an internship; Carter Phillips and his wife two rows ahead, and next to them the Thompsons.

The mood was joyful as Annie and Martin stepped down the aisle. Then Jon's parents, followed by Peggy and Alex, Sarah's sister, and finally Sarah, who looked breathtakingly beautiful wearing a simple silk satin dress with beaded chiffon appliques at the shoulders and a simple V-wrap front with an inset sash at the waist. She carried a bouquet of long-stemmed white calla lilies tied with raffia. Jon stood up front at the arbor, watching with wonder as she walked toward him. And Emily's eyes were drawn towards Thomas standing beside him.

The ceremony was simple as Emily had imagined it would be. Annie and Jon's mother both said a few words; the vows, written by Sarah and Jon, were exchanged; they were pronounced man and wife; a quick kiss and the crowd applauded. The steel band struck up a lively number as the wedding party and guests headed for the terraces. Smartly dressed waiters passed trays of hors d'oeuvres and glasses of sparkling champagne. Martin, his face the picture of love and pride, gave his father-of-the-bride toast that was both uproariously funny and amazingly touching.

The restaurant looked stunning. The glowing candles and twinkling chandeliers leant an air of romance. The pristine white linens were set with Christofle and Limoges, and the only color came from the burst of birds of paradise – vibrant orange, deep purple, touches of gold and red – that formed each table's centerpiece.

Emily had been amazed at the food last

year when she visited the Bluffs, and tonight's was even better. The chef, Jean-Pierre Rozan, known for the subtle blending of French, Caribbean and Asian flavors, had created the menu and supervised the cooking of the dinner, but only that. Having been at the Bluffs for over fifteen years, he was considered part of the family, and tonight he was a guest. As were Nelson and Johnno, the resort manager, both of whom were having a hard time not reverting to their daytime selves and overseeing the staff. 'No you don't, Nelson,' Emily heard Annie say at one point when Nelson started to organize the dinner service.

'I just had to check – there are so many new faces here. I know we trained them, but in such a short time. Maybe—'

'Tonight you are a guest. And Dawid is keeping a close eye, so please come and enjoy yourself.'

Sarah and Jon did not want a formal head table so the young crowd again sat together, although tonight there were several tables of them. Sarah and Jon were popular on the island and both of them also had a number of friends from New York. They had met in Manhattan and Jon had gotten his start there as a chef. Sarah had never really taken to the city, not to live in, anyway. But they were both excited to be returning for their honeymoon. The talk was livelier than last night and Sarah was pleased to see that Thomas was more relaxed and a part of things. He and Jon and a few of the others told funny stories of their growing up. They were quite the crowd, daring and occasionally reckless, although it was Thomas who always seemed to have had the more serious side. Thomas talked about their early morning sailing trip, looking lovingly at Emily. And it was clear that the others had noticed when Peggy leaned over at one point and whispered to her, 'Hmmm, you're right, the story does seem to be coming along.'

Annie introduced Emily and Peggy to Christiaan and Katrien Van Meeterens, Ariana's parents. Katrien was tall and pretty, with hair that must have once been blonde but was now pure silver. Christiaan was tall also; it was easy to see where Ariana's long legs came from. Katrien seemed quiet and a bit reserved, while he was more animated and full of laughter. They were friendly and easy-going and Emily immediately felt comfortable with them.

'Ariana is wonderful. She's been such a godsend,' Peggy told them. 'She's so good with children. Maggie loves her already; she barely bothered to wave goodbye when I was leaving her this afternoon.'

'Oh, she's just great with kids,' Christiaan said proudly. 'They'll miss her when she heads to college.'

'I bet you'll miss her too,' Emily said, thinking back to that time when her brother and sisters had headed off. 'Do most of the kids leave the island for college?'

'Many of them. Some even leave for high school,' Katrien said a little sadly. 'But it will be good for Ariana to see something beyond the island. We're headed to the States at the end of the week to look at colleges. She's a good student; she has lots of choices. It's time for her to go ... And after all, it's not forever.'

'No, Kat, you're right. Look at Jon and Sarah,' Annie said. 'And I get the sense that Alex is thinking about coming home. So it's certainly not forever.'

As the night went on, the music got louder and the crowd livelier – a decidedly more spirited evening than most at the Bluffs. Martin, an avid dancer, danced with half the women in the room, doing a mean tango with Marietta, a spirited foxtrot with Sarah and a gallant waltz with Nora. Annie moved from table to table, gracious as always, making sure that everyone was enjoying themselves. Emily discovered that Thomas was a great dancer and the two of them danced all night. At midnight, when the DJ came on and the disco balls dropped from the ceiling, the room shook to the beat of the drums.

Peggy was one of the first to leave, stopping to say goodnight to the Van Meeterens. 'I hope I didn't stay too late,' she said. 'Shall I have Ariana walk up and meet you here?'

'No,' Katrien answered somewhat enigmatically. 'Teenagers are complicated creatures. Ariana has a friend picking her up.'

Emily and Thomas left soon after, exhausted now and anxious to be together. Tonight, as they walked down to the beach, their hands tightly entwined, they rehashed the day, relishing the time with friends but also their early morning sail together. 'What a perfectly wonderful day,' Emily said. 'So much joy. I never want it to end.'

Thomas was quiet for a moment and then, turning towards Emily and looking deeply into her eyes, he murmured, 'I could stay.'

She held his gaze, and her heartfelt response, when it came, was almost a whisper. 'I'd like that, Thomas.'

SEVEN

Bzzz ... bzzz ... bzzz. Emily awoke groggy and couldn't figure out where the sound was coming from. For a moment she ignored it and, looking sleepily over at Thomas, she allowed herself to savor thoughts of last night. Bzzz ... Bzzz. She looked around her, her dark blue dress lying on the floor, Thomas' suit jacket on the chaise. Bzzz ... bzzz. She looked at the clock on the night-stand, its green numbers glowing: 6:45 a.m. The persistent buzzing kept intruding and she sat up, rubbing her eyes. On the table was Thomas' cell, vibrating loudly.

'Thomas,' she said, shaking his shoulder. 'Thomas, it's your cell.'

Thomas woke immediately, sitting up and running his hand through his hair. He look-ed as if he wasn't sure where he was. 'My cell? Uh oh, my cell. This is never a good sign.'

'Moller,' he said, already starting to pick

up his clothes. 'Moller here.'

This was followed by a number of 'uh huh's' and a final, 'OK, I'll be there in fifteen minutes.'

Putting down the phone, he immediately started to get dressed. 'Sorry, Emily, I have to go.'

'What's wrong?'

'That was my assistant. There's been a ... a body washed up on Manchebo Beach. A young girl.'

By the time Thomas drove the ten miles from the Bluffs to Manchebo Beach there was a crowd already assembled. 'Move everyone back,' he ordered, taking command of the situation. 'I want everyone off this beach.' Although early, the sun was already hot and Thomas could feel the sweat soaking the back of his shirt. The beach was swarming with police. Revolving red and blue lights formed a perimeter around the body and a detective was circling it, taking pictures from every angle.

He walked over to the officer who had called him. 'What do we have, Hendricks?'

'Not much. Body must have washed up early this morning. Found by those two kids over there.' Thomas looked over to see the kids, a boy and a girl, ten or eleven – they looked to be pretty shaken. 'Tall, probably about five-nine or five-ten; young, maybe seventeen, eighteen; wearing white linen pants and a light green halter top, definitely expensive. Can't be sure of the cause of death, not till the ME gets a look, but I don't think she was in the water too long. Oh, and she was wearing a gold bracelet, engraved. There's a name on the inscription – Emily.'

For a moment, Thomas was struck by the name, but he didn't have time to dwell on it. 'OK, I'm going to talk to the kids. You start with the usual. Have them check the airlines, all the manifests, begin with the past week then go backwards. Look for any missing persons report and call the embassies. Check out any Emily that you find.'

Thomas walked over to the two kids seated now on the sea wall at the edge of the beach. He bent down to be on their level and spoke slowly and softly. 'I'm Inspector Moller,' he said, putting out his hand to the boy. 'What's your name?'

'Kiko,' the boy answered, his dark brown eyes wide and his hand shaking a bit.

'Con ta bai, Kiko?' He asked in Papiamento, the most common language spoken on the island, trying to put the boy at ease.

'OK,' the boy answered.

'Is this your sister?'

The boy shook his head up and down. The sister, obviously younger than the boy, stared straight ahead, not even looking at Thomas.

'What's her name?'

'Dury.'

'Bon dia, Dury, con ta bai?' At that, the little girl started to cry.

The kids didn't really have much to share. They came down to the beach first thing. Their mother worked the early shift at the Bucuti resort hotel right here on Manchebo Beach, and on school holidays like this one they'd come to work with her and spend their day on the beach. When they came down this morning, they saw the girl and thought she might be asleep. The boy bent down to shake her but she didn't wake up. They ran back to tell their mother.

'Was there anyone else on the beach?'

The boy just shook his head, no.

After the two kids, Thomas interviewed the mother and several of the workers at the hotel, always asking the same question: had they seen anyone?

One worker, an older man who washed dishes in the kitchen, thought he saw two beach tennis players coming up from the other end of the beach, closer to Eagle Beach a mile or so to the north, but only from a distance so he couldn't really give a description. Another thought she saw a maintenance worker by the sea wall at the Bucuti resort when she was arriving at work, but also from a distance and she didn't really pay any attention. Thomas had two of his men continue the interviews; there would be a lot more of them to do, but the ME had arrived so he headed back towards the water's edge.

Jan Van Trigt was a crusty old doctor who had started out as a family physician in the city of San Nicolas. The island's second largest city, located at the southern end, it was known for its nighttime entertainment. The area had gained a reputation for petty crime and drugs. Here Van Trigt had experienced the seamier side of island life. He had been the medical examiner for almost twenty years and was known for being thorough, but blunt and often brusque. He had almost finished his examination when Thomas walked over.

'Not much here. Probably wasn't in the water more than three or four hours, but she was dead when she went in. Didn't drown – strangled, I think, judging by the marks on her neck – although there's also a bump on the back of her head and some bruising on her face and arms. Can't be sure till I do the full autopsy. I'd say some sort of struggle and we'll need to test for drugs and alcohol. Young, blonde, five-nine, weight, maybe one twenty, one twenty-five. That's all I've got for now. Your man got enough pictures?'

'Just need the print guy to finish up,' Thomas said. 'Then we can move her.'

A few minutes later an ambulance with a flashing orange light made its way across the sand. The body was quickly removed and Thomas waited while the barriers were erected and his men began a painstaking search of the area for clues. There wasn't much more he could do here, so he left Hendricks in charge and headed back to the police headquarters.

Tensions were high when he got there. News of the body's discovery had leaked out and Thomas was greeted by a scrum of reporters. 'No comment,' he said several times to the shouted questions until finally he had to give them something. 'Listen, we have no comment at this point,' he shouted with some frustration. 'We're in the very early stages of this. It will certainly be an ongoing investigation. We hope to make a brief statement in about an hour or two. But please let us get on with our work.' Thomas was known as a straight shooter among the press; they accepted his word and stepped back to let him through.

'OK, what do we have?' he asked the sergeant when he got inside.

'Well, no missing persons report with the name Emily, and nothing from any of the embassies. We have three Emilys from the airline manifests this past week: an Emily Lawrence from the UK, an Emily Jones from Miami and an Emily Harrington from New York.'

Thomas was stunned to hear her name, even though he'd known it would come up. 'You can forget the Harrington one, but try to track down the others. Were they heading to hotels or visiting friends?'

'One to a hotel, one to friends. We're sending men to both addresses.'

Thomas headed into his office and for a moment stared at his desk. Her name was Emily, he thought – how strange. Just then his phone rang.

'The deputy commissioner's on line one,' Millard said. Then, hearing Thomas's quiet groan, 'I could say you're not back yet.'

Thomas knew how lucky he was with the men who worked under him. He, Hendricks,

Millard and Keary had worked together for several years. Thomas had selected them himself and pushed hard for the commissioner to assign them to homicide. On really serious cases, like this one, Thomas felt they could almost read each other's minds. 'Thanks but ... no. Put him through.'

'Sorry, sir,' Millard said.

Thomas already knew what this would be about. Over the last ten years Aruba had had several of these cases. They hadn't gone well and there had been a huge amount of press and a lot of criticism of the local police.

'What have you got for me, Thomas?'

'Not much, sir,' Thomas answered. 'Body of a young girl washed up on Manchebo Beach. Van Trigt thinks she was dead before she went into the water, but we'll know more after the autopsy. No ID yet—'

'We can't afford another one of these cases, Thomas.' His voice was clipped and sharp. 'The commissioner is already getting calls. Your men have got to move on this. Find out who she is, what the hell happened down there and who did it. And find out quickly.' He hung up the phone.

'OK, have them go back another week on those manifests,' Thomas said to Millard. 'Anything on the fingerprints yet?'

'Too soon and not likely. She didn't look like someone who would be in the system, the clothes, the jewelry—'

'The jewelry. That's right – that's where you got the name. Get me that bracelet.'

EIGHT

It was a simple gold bangle about half an inch thick, no adornments on the front. Inside, however, was the inscription. *To Emily, All my love, Michael.* He knew as soon as he saw it. It must be hers ... *All my love, Michael.* For a moment he wondered what it meant. Why had she brought it with her? He thought their relationship had ended months ago. Had he been wrong or was it Emily who was confused? Too many questions, but he didn't have time to think about that now. With a dark scowl, he dropped the bracelet on his desk.

'You can stop looking for Emilys,' he said somewhat harshly to a bewildered Millard. 'I don't think this bracelet belonged to the girl. If I'm not wrong, I know the person who owns it.'

'But it was found on the body. How did it get there? She must have—'

'I don't know, but that's something we

need to find out. Damn, and that was our only real lead at this point. Back to square one. Anything from the ME?'

'Not yet,' Millard replied. 'Want me to call over there?'

'No, I'll walk over. Meanwhile, get a couple of more men over to Manchebo. I want everyone interviewed, and I mean everyone – every guest, every worker. Someone must have seen something. Check out those beach tennis players. A lot them play down there on Eagle Beach. It's right next to Manchebo Beach and they all know each other. See if you can track them down. And I want the CCTV footage from every hotel and store down there. Set up a team to start reviewing them.'

Thomas walked over to the morgue. He needed some time to think. Emily's bracelet. How had the dead girl ended up wearing that? He had to find out. Find something. The press was going to be all over this and, at this point, the police had nothing. For now, he wanted to keep news of the bracelet quiet. At least until he knew what they were dealing with. As soon as it came out, this case would involve Emily and he wasn't ready for that. Could she possibly have known this girl? Or maybe she had sold the bracelet? Given it away? He had to get some answers. He'd head to the Bluffs as soon as he'd spoken to the ME again.

'Ah, Thomas. Impatient as ever, I see. Come in. Just finished.'

Thomas hated going into the morgue. It was cold and stark, all stainless steel and sharp, medicinal smells.

'I don't have much more for you,' Van Trigt said. 'Definitely dead before she went into the water. Lungs are dry. The blow to the back of the head is superficial, as is the bruising. But the marks on the neck are consistent with manual strangulation. Stomach contents show she ate not too long before she died. I've taken all the samples. We'll send them out for testing. Definitely some alcohol, maybe drugs, who knows?'

'Any thoughts as to where she was dropped in the water?'

'Hmmm, could have been anywhere. Hard to know, given the tides. Could have been right nearby or further down the coast. We don't even know what time she washed up there, but check the time of the incoming tide – that should give us some idea.'

The young girl's body lay face-up on the slab, all but her head covered with a sheet. Thomas took a step closer and looked.

Startled, he reached out a hand to touch her face but immediately drew it back. He knew right away. He had seen this girl. Where was it? Last night, after the wedding? No, the night before. My God, he thought, the young girl who was minding the baby. How could that be? That beautiful young girl they had said goodnight to on Friday. He had met the parents at the wedding reception last night. Lovely couple, friends of Annie and Martin, but for the life of him he couldn't remember their names.

'Thanks, Jan. I'm afraid we have a lot to do on this one.'

'When don't we,' Jan said with a shake of his head.

Thomas headed out to the street, pulling out his phone as he walked back to head-quarters. 'Millard, I think I may have a lead on who this girl is. If I'm right, and I think I am, get ready. We'll have a firestorm on our hands. I'll call when I know more.'

His next call was to the Bluffs. 'Martin, it's Thomas. I don't know if you've heard yet but—'

'We've just heard. It's already been on the news. A girl on Manchebo Beach,' Martin said. 'A young girl, they said. Do you know anything, Thomas? I can't believe this has happened again. Young girls. It's so sad and terrible for the island to have another one of these cases. It's going to hurt us.'

'That's not the worst of it, Martin. I'm on my way over. I need to talk to you and Annie.'

'I see,' Martin said, his voice strained. 'We're here. Come straight to the house.'

NINE

Annie and Martin were in the living room of their house, a beautiful old villa on the northwest corner of the island that housed six large guest rooms below their own private living space, when Thomas arrived, still wearing his clothes from the night before but now wrinkled and sweaty. It was obvious from his face that this was very bad news.

'Thomas, what's wrong?' Martin asked, sensing that this somehow involved the Bluffs. Annie sat beside him, her eyes quiet and anxious, her hands in her lap slowly twisting round and round each other.

'I recognized the girl, Martin. That's why I'm here.'

Martin's thoughts immediately went to the night before. All those young people at the wedding; everyone having such a good time. Could it be possible? One of the guests? They had all been drinking, of course, but Martin had made certain that everyone was

OK leaving. He had checked to make sure that there were designated drivers. The roads could be treacherous on a dark night. But how? The body was found on the beach. It wasn't a car crash. Perhaps someone had stopped at the pier. An accident, a fall.

'Those friends of yours at the wedding, the parents of the girl minding Peggy's baby?' Thomas continued.

'The Van Meeterens, but what could they have to do with this?'

'I'm sure that the girl ... the girl on the beach was their daughter.'

'Their daughter ... but their girls are both away at school,' Annie said, looking puzzled. 'How could...' Then she realized what Thomas was saying. 'Ariana? No, Thomas.' Annie jumped up from her seat. 'Please tell me that's not true.' Her voice shook and her eyes begged him to be mistaken.

'That's just not possible, Thomas.' Martin's voice held a trace of anger. 'Ariana was at the Bluffs last night. She was minding Maggie.'

'I'm sorry,' Thomas said. 'I recognized her from when I saw her on Friday night after the rehearsal dinner. Emily and I were heading down to the beach and the girl, Ariana, was heading for the main entrance. I knew as soon as I saw her this morning at the ... I'm so sorry. We'll need a formal ID, of course, but ... I'm sure.'

Annie tried to speak but all that came out was a muffled cry. She put her hands up to her face and wept. Martin went over and put his arms around her, and for a few moments they said nothing. Finally, Annie looked over at Thomas.

'My God, do Christiaan and Kat know?' she asked.

Thomas shook his head. 'No. I couldn't remember their names so no one knows yet. I had to talk to you. I'll have to let the deputy know and then I'll have to head over there to break the news.' It was in moments like these that Thomas hated his job. How to tell parents that their beautiful daughter was dead, senselessly murdered? The sheer horror of it was almost unimaginable.

'I'd like to help,' Annie said, wiping the tears from her face. 'Kat and I have been good friends since Martin and I moved here. May I come with you?'

'Of course, Annie. I'm sure having you there would mean a great deal. But there's something else.' Thomas paused, not even sure how to say what must follow. 'Ariana was wearing a gold bracelet, a bangle. There was an inscription inside. It read, *To Emily, All my love, Michael.*'

Martin and Annie looked astounded. 'What are you...' Annie hesitated. 'How is that possible? Have you—'

'I have to speak to Emily,' Thomas said, averting his eyes. 'And Peggy. I need to speak to her too.'

'Of course,' Martin said with a deep sigh. 'I'll walk down and get them.'

'I'll go with you, Martin,' Annie added. 'I don't want you to walk alone.'

TEN

Emily had showered and dressed as soon as Thomas left. She had been stunned by his news. She didn't really want to see anyone, not sure if she should say anything about the call, so she made coffee in the suite and ate a couple of pieces of leftover fruit. For a long while she just sat looking out the window at the bay beach. Somehow it looked different now, quiet and deserted. The morning was overcast and the air humid. Emily knew that there would probably be rain soon, a quick shower that would blow over, but she could not stay in her suite any longer. She decided to take her book and sit outside.

She settled herself in the lounge chair and tried to read, but with little success. She couldn't help thinking about Thomas, but not in the way she had envisioned. She imagined him in his car racing to the crime scene, all thoughts of last night overshadowed by the horror of what lay ahead of him.

Gone would be the lightness, the laughter they had enjoyed. Would it be lost forever? she wondered. Swallowed up by the sight of the young girl's body.

After a while Peggy and Maggie emerged from their room. 'So ... how was your night?' Peggy said with a mischievous grin. 'Thought you'd be sleeping in this morning.'

For a moment Emily allowed herself to think of the pleasure of last night, but only for a moment. She honestly didn't know how to answer Peggy, so she settled for a subdued, 'It was great.'

'Not the rousing response I expected,' Peggy said, looking at Emily suspiciously.

'The wedding was great fun,' Emily went on. 'Thomas and I had a ball. How was Maggie when you got back to the suite?'

'Sound asleep and she slept all night but, as always, she was up at seven. Ariana is terrific. I'm hoping she's coming this afternoon for a few hours. I'd love to do some snorkeling and Annie said there was a group going out to Baby Beach. It's all the way over at the other end of the island and I hear the sea life is amazing. You should come along ... unless you have other plans?' There was that grin again.

'No plans. Not so far, anyway.'

Peggy tried to distract Maggie with her pail and shovel, but Maggie was restless and the humid air had brought out the tiny beach gnats. 'Want to take a walk?'

'I'd love to,' Emily said, dropping her book on the lounge chair. A walk would be perfect, she thought.

'I haven't seen the ocean beach yet. I hear it's beautiful and we might catch a breeze there.'

They put Maggie in the stroller and headed along the garden path that led down a few steps and curved to open up at the ocean beach. There was almost no one out and the main house looked deserted as they passed. Peggy kept up a lively conversation, jumping from comments about the wedding guests to Sarah and Jon, to stories of home. Emily said little, her thoughts invariably drifting back to last year. In the distance she heard church bells ringing. Sunday morning, she thought.

The ocean, when they reached it, was roiling, its usually blue waters reflecting the grey of the sky and its giant waves crashing against the beach. 'It's magnificent,' Peggy said as the winds picked up. 'Sarah told me about what happened here last year. She was so worried at the time ... Oh, Emily, I'm sorry. I should have thought. You probably have awful memories of—'

'That's OK, Peggy.' For a moment Emily's thoughts returned to that horrifying day when she had found Roger Stirhew's body on the ocean beach. She could see it so clearly and felt a shiver down her spine at the memory. 'But you're right, I do have awful memories. Let's head back before the rain starts.'

They had just about reached their rooms when they saw Martin and Annie coming towards them.

'Morning,' Peggy said brightly, then saw their faces.

They both looked terrible, pale and worn, and Annie had obviously been crying.

'What's wrong?' Emily asked, sure that this had something to do with Thomas's early morning call.

'We need both of you to come up to the main house. We'll explain there,' Martin answered. Annie just stood there, her face like stone. No one spoke as they walked up the path.

Thomas was waiting when they got there. 'Thomas?' Emily said, her voice wary.

'Emily.' Thomas came towards her, his arms outstretched as if to hug her. But then he remembered why he was there, thought of the bracelet and dropped them to his side. 'Please, both of you, come and sit down.'

Emily and Peggy sat down on the couch. Maggie started to squirm and whimper as if she sensed the tension in the room. 'I'll take her,' Annie said, quietly picking her up out of the stroller.

'I'm afraid I have some bad news,' Thomas began. 'This morning the body of a young girl was washed up on Manchebo Beach. Emily knows this because she was with me when the call came in.' At first, Peggy looked shocked, and then she looked at Emily as if to say *now I understand*.

'Just a short time ago, I discovered the girl's identity. I hate to have to tell you this, but the girl is Ariana Van Meeterens.'

'No,' Peggy said, looking from Thomas to Martin and Annie. 'That can't be. She was here till ... how could that be?'

'Oh my God, Thomas,' Emily said. 'That lovely young girl ... but what happened?'

'We don't know much yet, but we know she didn't drown. She was strangled before she went into the water.'

All of them were shocked to hear this. Martin put his head in his hands and Annie started weeping again. Peggy went over to her and gently took Maggie. 'Oh, Annie,' she said. 'I'm so sorry. I know how fond you were of her.'

'We have very little to go on,' Thomas continued. 'Her parents don't know yet, but there is one very strange thing.' He turned to look at Emily and she noticed a question in his gaze. 'She was found wearing a gold bangle with an inscription inside: *To Emily, All my love, Michael.*'

Emily gasped, 'My bracelet, but how...?'

'I'm hoping you can help me with that. It is your bracelet, Emily?'

'It must be. I brought it with me. It was a gift ... from Michael.' She felt an overwhelming need to explain – not to the others, but to Thomas. 'He gave it to me years ago,' she continued, her eyes almost pleading with his. 'I wanted him to take it back but he wouldn't.'

'When did you last see it?' His eyes were still searching her face.

'I can't remember. I remember grabbing my bangles from the dresser at home at the last minute. They were gold and I was going to wear gold with my aqua dress...' She knew she was rambling but couldn't seem to stop herself. 'I did it without even thinking. Well, anyway, when I got here I put all my jewelry in the box on the dresser in my suite. I haven't worn it. I haven't even looked for it. I thought ... but surely Ariana ... how could she have—'

'I don't know. That's something we'll have to figure out. Was Ariana in your room at all?'

'No.'

'Was there any sign that someone could have been in your room when you weren't there? After all, there are no locks on the doors ... anyone could have gotten in. Was there any sign ... things out of place, anything else missing?'

'Oh, Thomas, stop,' Annie called from the other side of the room, her voice and her eyes angry. 'Please, stop. You're not saying that Ariana would have—'

'Annie, I'm sorry, but I have to ask.'

'There was never any sign that someone was in my room,' Emily said brusquely. 'None at all.'

'Is all the rest of your jewelry there?'

'I don't know. I know my sapphire earrings are there; I wore them last night. But I didn't put them back in the box. I just left them on the dresser. I didn't look in the box.'

'OK, I'm going to ask you to go down to your suite and check. See if everything else is there and call up here and let me know. Perhaps last night during the wedding...' Thomas didn't finish his thought. 'Now, I need to talk to Annie and Martin, and then Annie and I have to head to the Van Meeterens'.'

Emily shuddered to think what that would be like. 'I'll check right now,' she said. 'And Annie, I'm so sorry.' She hugged Annie and then, turning to Thomas, said, 'I'll call up as soon as I've checked.'

'No need for you to stay, Peggy,' Thomas added. 'But I'll need you to think about the last two days. The time you spent with Ariana, was there anything ... *anything*. I don't even know what at this point, but please think about it.'

'Of course, but I don't ... I'll think about it. Wait, Emily, I'll walk down with you.'

They walked quickly back and Emily immediately went to the box on her dresser. 'It's all here, Peggy,' she said. 'My gold necklace, the earrings. Wait ... my other bangle. It's not here. How strange. I always wore the two of them together. The other one was a graduation gift from my parents. I loved it. It's not here either, but everything else is. I'll call Thomas.'

ELEVEN

The young man sat in a darkened room on Helfrichstraat, a small dingy street near the old oil refinery in San Nicolas, smoking cigarette after cigarette. The TV, its sound turned off, played before him. Over and over ran the scene at Manchebo Beach. He didn't bother to listen anymore; they just kept repeating the same thing. A beautiful young girl washed up, again and again.

That stupid girl, he thought. It was her own fault. What had she thought? That he was just going to let her tell? Even if he had wanted to, it was too late for him to get out of this. He was in too deep. What did she know? She was rich, rich and spoiled ... and pretty. She had been awfully pretty and sometimes when he was with her ... well, he could almost see himself as ... But it made no sense to think about that now. What did she know about anything? He had been so sure. He had been smart. Waited till she had

94

fallen for him. Bided his time until everything was set. How had it gone so wrong?

He got up and paced back and forth across the small space. He had to think. He had to go through everything in his mind. He had thought of leaving, of running away. But he had worked too hard to give this up. It meant everything. Money and connections. He would have to find another way.

OK, what to do now? He rubbed his hand through his straw-colored hair. He had to cover his tracks. Who had seen them together? They had spent a couple of hours doing tequila shots at Charlie's bar, but the place had been packed and there had been a crowd of them all drinking and dancing. He had always been careful – never seen with just her. Always one of the crowd. Some people might recognize her, but he didn't think anyone would think of them as a couple. After that they had headed to Palm Beach, but by then they were alone.

He knew she hadn't told anyone about him. She knew if her parents found out it would be over.

He had to think back carefully. Had anyone seen him when he met her on the path at the Bluffs on Friday evening? That had been stupid, so stupid, but he'd needed to see her. And he was just another worker. They had hired dozens of them. She'd been begging to see him and he'd had to get this settled. He'd spent only a few minutes with her trying to convince her to go through with his plan. Time was getting short and she had to agree. Just this once, he had promised her. Just to get me out of this jam. But she was wavering. 'Look, we can't talk about this now. Let's talk later,' he'd said, sure that he could convince her. 'I'll pick you up at the front gate.' She was leaving at the end of the week and it had to be now. It would have all worked out so well.

Had anyone seen him later when he picked her up? He was trying to remember. He had watched as she headed to the entrance. She had stopped to talk to a couple; the woman had red hair. She had gestured towards the car. He had already ditched that. Could they have seen him? Had he had the inside light on? He couldn't remember.

And the stupid bitch with the kid? Ariana couldn't stop talking about them, especially the kid. Drove him crazy. Had she noticed him on the path Friday evening? Probably not. He was just another worker. He wasn't with Ariana at that point and she had walked by pretty quickly. He had looked away. He didn't think she'd paid any attention, but now he couldn't be sure.

He knew no one had seen him last night after the wedding. There was no one around when he picked her up and he had been more careful, waiting a little further down the road from the front gates.

He turned the sound up – an announcement. So they knew who she was. Not much else. No talk about witnesses. He'd have to be sharp now. He'd have to pay close attention. He didn't think anyone had seen him, but if they had, the redhead or the kid's mother, could they identify him? He knew he couldn't take that chance. Whatever happened, he'd be keeping a careful eye on them.

TWELVE

Emily watched from Reception as Annie was dropped off. She had hoped Thomas would come in, but no. Annie looked awful, her face grey, her eyes red.

'Oh, Emily,' she said, coming up the steps. 'You can't imagine.' And her tears started to fall.

'Annie, I wish there was something ... I'm so sorry,' Emily said, putting her arms around Annie, whose sobs were now uncontrollable. 'You should head up to the house. Martin's in the office; I'll tell him you're back.'

Martin Maitland sat with his head in his hand as he held the phone to his ear. 'Yes, Thomas, I understand,' Emily heard him say as she entered.

'Annie's back, Martin. She's gone up to the house. Is there anything I can do?'

'Honestly, Emily, there's nothing anyone can do. I don't think I can face this again. I know it's awful of me to even be thinking about the Bluffs, but after last year? Now we're drawn into another murder.'

'But Martin, this isn't the same at all. The Bluffs had nothing to do with this. Why...'

'You don't understand, Emily. Don't you see? Ariana was here last night ... and your bracelet. I just can't understand that. They'll want to question everyone. How did she get your bracelet? She wouldn't ... She couldn't have...'

'Martin, I...' But she couldn't think of anything more to say.

'Come,' Martin said. 'Come with me. I need to talk to Annie. She could use some support right now.'

Annie was sitting on the living-room couch, her feet drawn under her, her face empty. 'Martin,' she said, reaching her arms out to him. 'It was so horrible. I can't even ... Kat and Christiaan, what can I say? They're devastated. Couldn't even speak. Thomas did the best he could but...'

Emily knew Annie needed to talk.

'At first, they wouldn't even listen to Thomas. "This is not possible," Kat said over and over. "You're wrong," Christiaan insisted. "You've made a terrible mistake." He swore Ariana was upstairs, still asleep. He even went up to her room. Of course, she wasn't there. When he came down, Kat knew right away. She just kept screaming, "No, no, don't say it, Christiaan, don't say it." Then, begging, "Please, Christiaan, please don't say it." Her sobs and cries, the sound of it...'

'My God,' Martin uttered. 'I can't even imagine. I think of Sarah and Alex. What if...'

Annie was sobbing again. 'I tried ... I tried to help, to comfort Kat, but there was nothing ... nothing.' Her voice dropped to a whisper. 'And then, when Thomas mentioned the bracelet, they became so angry. Kat just looked at me and walked out of the room, and Christiaan asked ... told us to leave. I can't talk about it anymore. I have to lie down.'

'Yes, lie down. We'll talk more later.' Martin led Annie out of the room.

'Is there anything we need to...' Emily heard Annie mumble.

'Nothing, nothing right now,' Martin answered, his voice quiet. 'Just sleep for a bit, then we'll talk about everything.'

Emily just sat in the living room, not knowing what to do. She looked out at the veranda, the bright blue sky, the vibrant flowers, and wondered how everything could look the same as yesterday and yet be so utterly changed.

'What happens now?' she asked Martin when he returned.

He shuddered as he answered. 'There'll be a press conference shortly. Thomas will speak. He won't say much. No mention of the bracelet, not yet. And then they'll come here. I couldn't say that to Annie, not yet. God, if only this could be a bad dream.'

'Is there anything I can do?'

'No, nothing. You should go. Get some rest yourself. This will be hard on everyone. I need to talk to Nelson. Get the names of the staff working on Friday and Saturday.'

Emily headed back to her suite. Peggy was sitting on the sea wall while Maggie played in the sand at her feet.

'You're back. I knocked on your door but—'

'I was up at Annie and Martins's. Annie's back; she's lying down.'

'Do they know anything?'

Emily just shook her head. 'There's going to be a press conference any minute now. I was going to watch from my room.'

'OK if I come?' Peggy asked, picking up Maggie.

'Sure. I could use some company.'

As soon as Emily turned on the TV and Peggy had settled Maggie on the floor with some toys, Thomas' face appeared on the screen. He looked tired and drawn as he spoke. Martin was right – there wasn't such to say. A body washed up on Manchebo Beach, the cause of death, Ariana's name and age, no suspects, no motive, and at the end an appeal for help. Anyone who had seen anything, please call. They showed a picture of her, one they must have gotten from her school or perhaps a friend. From what Annie said, Emily was sure that Thomas hadn't gotten a picture from her parents. She was looking straight into the camera. Khaki linen pants, a white shirt, her blonde hair blowing slightly in the breeze and a wide smile. It was heartbreaking to look at.

'How was Annie?' Peggy asked as the press conference ended.

'Terrible. The Van Meeterens were devastated. Who wouldn't be? But they were angry too – angry at Annie, and at Thomas.'

'But why? It wasn't—'

'Over the bracelet. Annie said they got incredibly upset when Thomas asked about the bracelet. Felt he was accusing Ariana of ... I can understand it of course, this whole thing must be so unreal, so tragic for them, but...' Just then Emily's cell phone rang.

'Hello?'

'Emily, it's—'

'Oh, Thomas. We just saw the press conference.' Peggy quickly picked Maggie up and headed out the door. 'How are you? Sorry, I guess that's a stupid question.'

'No, no. It's fine.' Thomas sounded exhausted. 'This is going to be a long, dreadful day. I'm headed to the Bluffs now, but I wanted to get a minute to talk to you before ... Could you meet me outside the front gate?'

'Of course. Anything.'

'I should be there in about fifteen minutes.'

'I'll be waiting.'

THIRTEEN

Thomas's car arrived as soon as Emily reached the front gate of the resort. She got in and he drove slowly up the road. 'I thought I would just pull up around the bend here so we could talk away from the house.' He looks haunted, Emily thought, and reached over to put her hand on his. For a moment he held it tightly, but then he dropped it and rubbed his eyes.

'Thomas, I wanted to explain ... about the bracelet ... I...'

'No need to explain, Emily.'

'No it's important ... to me. I want you to understand. That bracelet held some memories for me, but that's all ... just memories. That part of my life is over, you know that. When I picked up that bracelet to bring it with me, it was just a piece of pretty gold jewelry that would match my earrings. Nothing more.'

'I understand. I have to admit, I was a little

surprised when I first saw it, maybe more than surprised by how it was found, the connection to Ariana's death – maybe shaken more than surprised. But after hearing you talk about it earlier, I realized it was just a bracelet.' And for a moment, Thomas took her hand again.

'I spoke to Annie,' Emily said. 'She told me a little of what happened. It must have been awful for you, Thomas.'

'It was, always is. The press is going crazy already. We've had a couple of these cases – missing or murdered young women. They're the worst, really. Reporters digging up every last bit of dirt. Screaming headlines. I hate them. I know it's their job to report the news, but do they have to ... I don't know, it just seems they enjoy it so damn much. And we didn't do so well on those earlier cases. I was just walking a beat at that time, but I remember what it was like.'

He grew quiet, just sat staring out the front window. Emily waited a couple of minutes then tried to draw him back. 'What happens now, Thomas?'

'Uh. Well, we have teams of detectives out. There's a ton of people to talk to. Family, although we'll wait a bit before going back to the Van Meeterens, try to give them a little more time. But we can't give them too long – we need information. We have so little to go on. Then friends, schoolmates, anyone who might have seen Ariana last night. We're combing the Manchebo Beach area, but nothing so far. We'll interview half the island before this is over.'

'And here at the Bluffs?' Emily asked.

'That will start now. I've spoken to Martin already. We have a team coming over. Myself and two detectives, which is all we can spare right now. We have to interview everyone – guests, staff. Martin's making up a list. The thing that keeps getting to me is your bracelet. How did she get it? I had to ask the Van Meeterens about it.'

'I know. Annie told me.'

'I knew they'd be angry but ... we have to know. Had they seen it before? Did she steal it? I know that's hard to imagine, but it wouldn't be the first time someone steals something that they could easily buy – Ariana's parents are pretty rich and I'm sure if she wanted something like that ... but sometimes people do steal for ... well, it happens. If not, if she didn't take it ... then someone had to have given it to her. I guess it would have been pretty easy for someone to walk into an unlocked room and target the jewelry box ... but why?' Thomas banged his fist on the steering wheel. 'I'm sure you have been thinking about this. Is there anything?'

Emily just shook her head.

'Well, we'd better head back. I have a lot of work ahead of me.'

Annie and Martin were both in the office when they arrived at the main house. Annie looked a little better, but not much. They were poring over a long list of names.

'I've almost finished the list, Thomas,' Martin said with resignation. 'The wedding guests are easy. There are a lot of them, about a hundred and thirty, but about eighty of them are staying here at the Bluffs, and I've given you addresses and phone numbers for the others. A number are people from the island, some elected officials, the others resort owners.'

'Thank you, Martin,' Thomas said, reaching his hand out for the list. 'I know this can't be easy.'

'The staff,' Martin continued. 'I'm afraid the staff is a different matter. You know that we hired a lot of extras for the two days. Some of them we knew, but not all. Nelson is working on that list. He should have it for you shortly. Our regulars are fine. Do you want to interview them here?'

'We'll do as many of the interviews here as we can. It'll save us some time.'

'I've asked everyone to assemble in the dining room at noon,' Martin said, getting up from his chair. 'I thought it best that you speak to them all at once. Let them know what's happened, although I'm sure most of them know already. And explain about the interviews. Is there anything else for now?'

Thomas looked intently at the list. 'Quite some list. I knew it would be. Some of these people won't be too happy with the idea of being interviewed.'

'Probably not – especially your chief.' Martin smiled for a moment, but almost immediately a look of sadness and resignation returned. Then, looking at the clock, 'Well, I think we should head down.'

'Oh, one last thing, Martin,' Thomas said. 'Still no mention of the bracelet, please, not yet. I don't know how long we'll be able to keep it quiet but, for now, we're saying nothing.'

The four of them made their way to the dining room where the assembled guests and most of the staff milled around. The room immediately became quiet as they walked in and Martin, Annie and Thomas made their way to the podium.

Emily chose to stay at the back of the room, and as Martin spoke she looked around her. It was hard to imagine that same podium had been used less than twenty-four hours ago for charming speeches and congratulatory toasts. Martin himself had stood there talking about his joy at Sarah and Jon's marriage. The dining room was very different today. The tables were empty and the bowers of hydrangea and roses had been removed. Only the birds of paradise centerpieces stood, forlorn looking, in the center of the bare tables.

It was obvious that most of the guests had heard about the murder of the young girl on the island, but few of them realized the connection to the Bluffs and most reacted with shock at the news. Martin did his best to speak calmly and without emotion, but a number of the guests were friends of the Van Meeterens and others had met them last night at the wedding. Emily could see people responding with gasps and tears. 'Please, I know how upsetting this is. As many of you know, Katrien and Christiaan are close friends of ours and Ariana was...' At this, Martin's voice broke. He stepped back from the podium and Thomas took over.

'I know this has been disturbing and difficult for many of you. I just want to say a few words about next steps. I'm sure you realize that, as far as we know right now, Ariana was last seen here at the Bluffs last night. We will be interviewing each of you.' At this he put up his hand. 'I know your first reaction is "I don't know anything" and that may be true. But I would ask each of you to think about the last two days. Ariana was here both last night and the night before. She was also here for a couple of hours on Friday afternoon. So if you saw her, we need to know about it, and most importantly, if you saw anyone with her. Beyond that, if you saw anything or anyone that you thought odd or strange, maybe not at that moment, but possibly thinking back now.'

A woman in tennis whites raised her hand. 'I don't really even know who she is, or what she looked like, so how could I know if I saw her?' she said, sounding petulant. Emily could see Annie turn toward her with a look of disdain, while Thomas ignored her.

'We have flyers which the two detectives, Detective Hendricks and Detective Keary,' he nodded towards the two men standing to his left, 'will hand out. Please take them with you as you leave. We'll be conducting interviews here at the main house. There will be a list of names and the order of the interviews posted at Reception. For now, I would ask Mr and Mrs Phillips, Mr and Mrs Blake, Ms St. John, Ms Richards and Mr and Mrs Weddington to meet us back here in fifteen minutes. I'd ask the rest of you to please check that list. Thank you.'

Thomas stepped away from the podium and Annie and Martin started to leave the room. Several guests stepped forward to hug Annie, but there were a couple of people who seemed put out by the upcoming interviews who approached Martin. Emily wasn't surprised to see Nelson immediately step in to respond to whatever questions or comments they might have, allowing Martin a clear passage out of the dining room. Many of the guests stood around, not quite sure what to do.

Emily made her way up to the front of the room to where Thomas was standing. 'Thomas?'

'Emily,' Thomas said, looking distracted. 'I meant to mention, we have men dusting your suite for fingerprints, so if you could wait a bit before returning that'd be great. We'll also be doing Peggy's suite.'

Emily was taken aback, although she

shouldn't have been. Of course they'd be checking her suite for prints, either Ariana's or someone else's. Somehow, though, the thought of Thomas' men in her suite while she was up here in the dining room seemed ... intrusive. Why hadn't he told her before-hand? He should have ... should have what? She knew her feelings were unfair, even ridiculous. It was clear that Thomas was consumed with the investigation, as he should be, but, for her, it was difficult to go from the Thomas of last night to the Thomas of today. And the bracelet hadn't helped.

'Of course. That's fine,' she said, trying to not let her feelings show. 'Will you be want-ing to speak to me?'

'Not until later this afternoon. You and Peggy. I'd better go ... I need to organize the interview rooms.' And with that he headed out.

Emily hadn't gone five steps when Mari-etta was at her side. 'Well, my dear, it seems that we're in for it again. Not that I should complain. That poor, poor child ... and her parents. I cannot bear to think about it. I've met them before, of course. Kat and Annie were very close. And to think she was here just last night. What could have happened? These young people today. I must say it puzzles me so. Whatever has happened to the world?'

'Oh, I don't think young people are all that different,' Emily said.

'No, no perhaps not. I remember ... oh, it's many years ago. A friend of my cousin, Andrea, was killed. A young girl. Sixteen. It was so awful. It took Andrea ages to get over it. A tragedy, of course, just like this. But it seems that in those days, well, people knew each other better. Young girls weren't running around by themselves, wearing skimpy shorts and those tank tops, leaving nothing to the imagination. Not that I'm suggesting this poor girl did, of course. Oh, I suppose I'm just being...'

Just then Nora joined them. 'Now, now, Marietta, don't get yourself into a state. We should be on time as Inspector Moller asked.'

'Of course, of course,' Marietta said, waving her hand in front of her face. 'It's gotten so warm in here, or is it just me? I know I have nothing to tell him. Why, I don't think I saw that poor child at all. Or *did* we see her at the beach yesterday – or was that Friday? Friday, I think. Nora, was that the young girl playing with the baby?' Her voice started to get higher, her words faster. 'Why, it must have been, Nora. You remember her, the tall girl with the blonde hair...' Marietta noticed that Nora was holding the flyer. 'Yes, yes, that's her. Such a pretty young thing. How perfectly awful, such a—'

Nora gently took Marietta's arm, leading her out of the dining room. 'Come, Marietta. I'm sure Inspector Moller will be waiting for us.'

'Yes, yes, but I must think. Nora, was there anyone else with her? Did we see anyone else? Could it be that there was someone, someone lurking ... Oh, it's all too awful...' Marietta continued as they left.

The dining room was almost empty now. Some people sat on the terraces, a number walked up to Reception to check the list and a few wandered down towards the beach. Emily was unsure what to do. Would they be finished in her suite? She would walk down that way; no sense hanging around here.

Funny, she thought, the Bluffs was just as crowded as yesterday, but it was eerily quiet. Voices were muted, guests seemed to walk slowly and, although there were people on the beach, there was no one splashing in the water. Emily behaved much like the rest, but with a heavier heart. She was happy to see Peggy and Maggie sitting in the sand outside their suite.

'Are they in your room?' Emily asked, joining them.

'They've been in there for a while,' Peggy said, and Emily noticed how tired she looked. 'I stayed at first. They had some questions. Was this my hat? How about those glasses? It was, I don't know, creepy. Anyway, Maggie started to get restless so they said we could wait out here. They'd come out if they had more questions. How'd it go in the dining room?'

'Pretty much as you would expect. People shocked, some upset. And there's always those few ... They've started the interviews.'

'And Thomas?'

'Thomas is ... Well, this all falls on him, so as you can imagine he's—'

'I'm sorry, Emily. Just when—'

But Emily cut her short. 'Why don't we see if they're finished in there? We could take Maggie for a walk. Thomas said they would not be talking to us until later this afternoon.'

The forensic guys were just finishing up when they reached the door to her suite, so Peggy grabbed the stroller and they walked up the path.

'Let's head out to the road,' Emily said. 'I'd love to get out of here for a bit.'

FOURTEEN

The green Corolla idled two hundred yards from the entrance to the Bluffs. The young man sat fidgeting in the front seat. He had turned the radio off; couldn't stand to listen to it anymore. So he just sat and watched the coming and goings at the Bluffs.

He knew the cops were there. Forensics, too. They must be going crazy inside. He could picture it and for a moment he laughed. He knew it wouldn't be long before they contacted him. He had dressed the part. Khakis and a white linen shirt. He'd look like all the rest of them. Meantime, he'd just sit and wait.

He wondered how much they knew. Not much, he bet. He watched as the occasional car pulled up, discharging a passenger or two outside the gate. Staff, he thought – the only ones dropped outside. He had been there close to an hour when he struck gold. Those two women, the redhead and the other one wheeling the stroller, walked out the gate and turned down the road. He knew right away who they were – the redhead from the other night and the kid's mother, but it was funny, seeing them now he felt like he had seen them someplace before, not here at the Bluffs but someplace else. In town, maybe? On the beach? Somewhere...

They walked slowly, talking, occasionally reaching down to the baby. He would have to watch from a distance. Where the hell were they going, anyway? There was nothing up there.

Peggy was surprised when the landscape changed as they made their way along the deserted road. 'Strange,' she said. 'I've been to the Bluffs several times, but I don't think I've ever walked this road. I guess I spent most of my time on the grounds or heading into Oranjestad to dine or shop. Have you seen Sarah's shop?'

'I have. She's very talented and last time...' But Emily didn't want to think about last time. 'Well, I got some lovely things.'

Peggy grew more and more pensive as they walked. 'What do you think happened, Emily?'

'It's so hard to know. A young girl – was

she with a stranger, or a boyfriend? It could have been anyone. I know Ariana was getting a ride after she left here on Friday night. Thomas and I met her on the path. I saw a car waiting for her at the front gate, but I was too far away to see what kind of car or who was in it. I just saw the headlights, really. I'm sure they'll look into that. I didn't see her on Saturday night. Did she say anything to you when you went back to your room?'

At first, Peggy just shook her head. But then she remembered. 'It's funny, though – when I was leaving the wedding I asked Kat if I should tell Ariana to meet them up at the restaurant. I assumed she was going home with them, and she said something odd. She said someone was picking her up and then said something like "teenagers are complicated creatures". I laughed at the time and agreed with her, but thinking back, I wonder.'

Emily could certainly understand what Kat was saying. She remembered her sisters' and her brother's teenage years. Of course, that was different – her mother's death had changed everything, all of them struggling to come to terms with it. But still, much of what she dealt with was typical teenage stuff – Jane's curfews, Kate's boyfriends, Brian's drinking. She had found herself constantly trying to find that balance between freedom and structure, and often failing.

'I remember my own teenage years,' Peggy said. 'I wasn't the easiest teenager; I was the type who challenged everything. I was probably a little spoiled. But I was the youngest and my parents had been through that any number of times. They took it all in their stride – either that or they were just tired,' she laughed, then sobered. 'I keep seeing her face, Emily.'

'That smile; it's hard to imagine that smile gone,' Emily said, remembering Ariana sitting in the sand playing with Maggie. Neither of them wanted to talk about it anymore, but they just couldn't let it go.

'And I keep feeling there's something I'm missing. I don't think I saw anyone with Ariana on the path, but ... I was only with them for a few minutes – you were at the rehearsal. Ariana had been walking Maggie around hoping she would fall asleep and she was looking pretty tired by then, and I headed in to get dressed. Oh, it's no use, but there's something...'

'Try not to think so hard, Emily. It'll come. Someone you saw? Something Ariana said?'

'I just don't remember.'

'Ted wants Maggie and me to come home. He wanted to arrange a flight this afternoon, but I don't think we can leave. Not until they have a better idea of what happened. I told him I'd ask Thomas about it.' Peggy struggled to find something else to talk about. 'The landscape here is so different,' she said as the road hugged the coast.

'The northern coast is very different. A little like the ocean beach at the Bluffs, but the further along you go, the more exposed it is to the Atlantic and the wilder it gets.' This was the uncultivated part of the island, barren and forlorn. Within minutes, the terrain became more and more desolate, just small hills and sand dunes, with the occasional towering rock formation. 'The beaches tend to be rocky and the waves are very rough. No one really comes here to swim.'

The wind started to pick up and Emily pointed out the twisted divi-divi trees bent in their usual direction. 'See the way they bend? It's from the trade winds. They call them Aruba's natural compass because they always point southwest.'

'It's so bleak here, no lush green bushes and colorful flowers – just scruff and cacti and those trees. It reminds me more of a moonscape than the tropics.' Peggy shivered.

'It is bleak,' Emily said. 'But strangely beautiful. You can almost see Venezuela in the distance. If you look closely among the rocks you'll see the most amazing blue-green lizards, and last time I spotted some wild donkeys. If you keep walking, you come to the strangest sight. A dirt path lined with white crosses and small coffins and, among them, hand-lettered signs saying, "Pray for us sinners", "At the hour of our death", and "Pray, pray". It's so poignant.'

'It sounds haunting.'

'It is, but at the end of the path is a small, mustard-colored chapel, simple and stark with little light and thick walls. Annie said it's called the Pilgrims Church and people of all faiths go there to meditate.' Emily trembled as she remembered her last visit to the chapel. There was nothing contemplative about it – the shots, the chase, the bat cave. And suddenly she wanted nothing more than to get away from the barren landscape around them. 'We should head back,' she said.

They walked back more quickly, both of them anxious to leave the starkness and isolation behind.

Neither Emily nor Peggy noticed the car

idling beyond the Bluffs but the young man was intently watching their return. He could sense their mood, the slumped shoulders and slightly bowed heads. For a moment, he considered getting out of the car and approaching them, asking for directions and trying to gauge if there was any glimmer of recognition in their eyes, but he knew that was too risky. In fact, maybe it was too risky to hang around here any longer.

As he drove off, his cell phone rang. 'Yeah,' he said quickly.

'Is this William Thomas Dunlop?' a deep voice asked. Right away he knew and changed the tone of his voice.

'Yes, it is,' he answered, trying to sound casual. 'Who's this?'

'This is Detective Keary of the Aruban police.'

'How can I help you, Detective?'

'We're interviewing all staff from the Island Bluffs resort and—'

'I'm not really a staffer there,' he said, sure they wouldn't fall for it but figuring it was worth a try. 'I was just a temp hired for an event.'

'We're aware of that, but we need to talk to you anyway. We'd like you to come out to the Bluffs this afternoon, around four.'

'Sure thing. Can I ask—'

'Come to the main reception area and someone will direct you.'

Two hours, he thought. He ran his fingers through his hair, trying to make it look less scruffy. His hands had begun to sweat and he slipped the phone back into his pocket. Can't have that, he thought, taking a bottle of small white pills out of the glove compartment. He quickly swallowed one, then another, and headed south. There wasn't enough time to go back to the apartment, so he headed to the Bugaloe on Palm Beach.

'Hey, Billy,' the bartender called as he entered. 'How you been? Haven't seen you for a while.' Tommy Duffy had worked at the Bugaloe for almost thirty years. He had come down from the States on a vacation and never left. His once-dark hair was streaked with grey and he had put on a few pounds, but he was a happy man. He knew everyone on the island and was always a good source of information.

'Been working down in San Nicolas, night shifts.' Billy had been bartending on the island for the last few years, although he had left his last gig about two weeks ago.

'Get you something?'

'Just a coffee.' He didn't dare have a drink.

He had to be sharp for this interview. 'How's everything here?'

'Police have been all over this place. You heard about the body?'

'Yeah, it's all over the news. Washed up not too far from here, they said.'

'Down on Manchebo. Rich girl. Real beauty from the pictures. Didn't recognize her though; she didn't hang out here.'

'Yeah. I've never seen her, but you know those kids, they're all over the place. They have any leads?'

'Don't think so. Seems like a real fishing expedition at this point. Questioned everyone here and all along the strip. Hear something's up at the Bluffs though. That's the last place she was seen.'

'Heard that.'

'Shame for the Maitlands. They're good people. You ever work there?'

'Picked up a day here and there, but you know me, I'm not really a resort type of guy. Give me a bar any day. More my kind of people.' Billy fished a couple of bucks out of his pocket but Duffy just waved it away.

'On us. You should stop around a little more often.'

'Thanks, Tommy. I will,' he said as he pushed away from the bar and headed out the door.

OK, so no one has mentioned seeing her after the Bluffs. Maybe his luck would hold. But he better not count on it. He'd start thinking about an alibi on the way to see this Keary guy.

FIFTEEN

When Peggy and Emily reached the gate, they were met by a large man wearing a dark suit who had security written all over him. He had a clipboard in his hand and an unmistakable bulge under his jacket.

'Excuse me, ladies, but are you guests here at the Bluffs?'

'We are,' Emily answered for both of them.

'Could I just have your names, please?'

'Peggy Lawson and Emily Harrington.'

He checked the list and smiled. 'Thank you, ladies. Just a precaution.'

Both a bit shaken, they stopped at the beach bar on the way back. Emily realized she hadn't eaten anything since the leftover fruit that morning. It was hard to imagine that was just six hours ago. It was after two now, and the smell of food made her stomach growl. There was no lunch being served in the dining room, and probably no dinner either. It was hard to imagine how Martin and Annie were going to carry on, but with all these guests they had to do something. Luckily, most of them were good friends so it was a little easier.

Peggy and Emily ordered salads and Maggie had a plate of peas and mashed sweet potatoes that she happily smeared in her hair. There were a number of guests here but the atmosphere was still subdued. Emily was surprised to see Nora sitting alone at a nearby table. When she waved, Nora came over to join them.

'Oh, Emily,' she said, 'it's just so awful. People lining up waiting to be interviewed, everyone wanting to get it over with, and the questions ... Poor Annie and Martin. I can't believe they have to go through all this again.'

'Have they finished with many of them?' Peggy asked.

'They seem to be going through them pretty quickly. I'm not surprised. No one seems to know anything, but still. I spoke with that Detective Keary. Such a nice young man. Of course, he asked if we had seen Ariana. Then they wanted to know if there was anyone with her. Well, I was pretty sure there wasn't. No one but your sweet little baby, Peggy.' At this, she reached over to rustle Maggie's hair and was rewarded with a big smile. 'And then, had I seen anyone strange? Such a hard question to answer. You know, when something like this happens, you start looking at everyone so differently.'

'I don't see Marietta,' Emily said. 'Is she still up at the main house?'

'Thank heavens, no. These things upset her so. She went to lie down. She was somewhat overwrought, poor thing. And, wouldn't you know, with everything going on both of us forgot her medication this morning. So we went straight back to our room and she took her pills and went to lie down. I thought I would come up here and sit so she would sleep. I should go back and check on her, though,' Nora said, getting up from the table.

'I think I'll head back too,' Peggy added. 'I'd like to see if Maggie will take a nap. Would love to lie down myself. How about you, Emily?'

'I don't think I could sleep. No, I think I'll head up to the main house. See how things are going.'

When Emily reached Reception there were several people waiting to be interviewed. Penny, usually so vivacious, sat calmly behind the desk with a copy of the list in front of her.

'I'm glad you stopped by,' she said. 'I was just going to send a message to your room. Inspector Moller would like to see you shortly. He just has one more interview. Would you mind waiting?'

Most of the guests sat quietly, but one woman paced back and forth, muttering to herself. She had dark brown hair, dyed, a pinched face and a sharp chin. 'Mind waiting, mind waiting. This is ridiculous. I've been waiting here for twenty minutes. What a waste of time ... I'll tell Martin when I see him ... if I see him.' The others ignored her and she turned to Emily. 'Do you believe this? I knew I never should have come. Martin will certainly hear from me.'

Emily did her best to ignore her also, but she persisted. 'I imagine you must be a friend of Sarah's? From New York?' she said, shaking her head as if in disapproval.

'Yes, I'm from the city. Are you a friend of the family?'

'No, of course not. I'm Martin's sister-in-law. I shouldn't be on a list, sitting here waiting for almost half an hour. I shouldn't have to wait. I saw that girl. I told Penny. It's an insult; I'm family. Oh, yes, Martin will hear

129

about this.'

'Please, Joanne,' called an attractive middle-aged woman sitting across the room. 'Don't you think Martin has enough on his mind? The last thing he needs is to hear from you.'

Joanne turned sharply on the woman. 'That's always been the way with you, Alice. It's always been Martin, Martin, Martin. Never Eddie. Even when he was sick. You didn't have—'

'Joanne, this is neither the time nor the place for—'

'I'll decide when it's the time and place to say what—'

Just then, Penny looked up from the list and called, 'Joanne Maitland.'

Well, that was fortunate, Emily thought, as Joanne finished with: 'We'll continue this later.'

Emily sat in an empty chair next to the woman whose name was Alice. 'I'm sorry about that,' Alice said. 'She's just so difficult to deal with. I'm Alice Burns, Martin's sister. And you are?'

'Emily, Emily Harrington.'

'Oh, of course. I didn't get to meet you at the wedding but Martin has spoken of you. Once again, sorry about that. God knows I try not to get into it with her, but it seems I'm not too successful. I should try to be more like Martin. Joanne was married to our younger brother, Eddie. As you could probably tell, she has issues. I knew it was risky for Martin to invite her, but he felt he had to. Didn't want to hurt her feelings.' She rolled her eyes. 'Feelings. Not sure she has those.'

Emily didn't quite know what to say. 'Families are always complicated,' was the best she could do.

'You're right about that. Joanne has been nothing but complicated for Martin. Eddie died over ten years ago. It was just so tragic. And Martin has spent the last ten years taking care of Joanne – or trying to. She doesn't make it easy, God knows. Good luck to that detective.'

'I'm sure it will be fine. It sounds like she saw Ariana?'

'Well, she said she did, but you can never be sure with Joanne. On the one hand complaining about being on the interview list but on the other getting enjoyment from the spotlight, no matter how small it might be.'

At that point, Penny came over to Emily. 'I'm afraid Inspector Moller is going to be a little longer than he thought. Do you want to go back to your room and I could let you know when he's finished?'

'No, no, it's fine. I'll just wait here.'

'There's some refreshments set up on the terrace,' Penny said.

Overhearing, Alice said to Emily, 'I could do with a cold glass of lemonade. Why don't you join me?'

The late afternoon had grown sunny and hot and they were happy to enjoy the shade and a cool drink. Below them they could see the bay beach and, although the mood of the resort was still quiet, a number of guests were stretched out on the lounges and hammocks. It was a pleasant scene but it couldn't shake Emily's mood.

'How are Martin and Annie doing?' Emily asked Alice.

'I haven't seen them in a couple of hours,' Alice answered. 'Martin seemed to be holding up fairly well but Annie is wrecked. Going to the Van Meeterens' this morning took a lot out of her. And now having to deal with all this.'

'There was a security man at the gate when I came back in,' Emily said. 'Police?'

'Private security. Martin arranged it. The police don't have that kind of manpower and Martin's so worried about reporters coming on the grounds. Having the police here is difficult enough, but I understand the local reporters are all over this and Martin's trying to protect the guests.'

'I haven't seen much of the coverage, just the news conference this morning.'

'It's been on the TV all afternoon. They've started dredging up everything about this poor girl – her school, her friends, stories, rumors. At this point they haven't come up with much, but it's really disturbing, interviewing these kids when they're obviously upset, cameras trained on a growing memorial on the beach, then more cameras trained on the Van Meeterens' front door. Their *front door* – it seems so cruel. Disgusting, really.'

'Do you know Christiaan and Kat?'

'Oh, I've met them many times. Kat and Annie have been friends for years. And both of their older daughters stayed with Joe and me during some of their college breaks. We live in the city and have the extra room. Such lovely girls.'

'And Ariana?' Emily asked quietly.

Alice looked pensive. 'Oh, I'd see Ariana when Joe and I came down here.' For a moment her eyes misted. 'We'd almost always go to the Van Meeterens' for dinner one night and maybe dinner in town together another.'

As they talked, Sarah and Jon appeared at the door to the terraces. 'Oh, Aunt Alice,' Sarah cried, tears flowing down her face as Alice hugged her.

'Sarah, what are you doing here?' Alice asked. 'You're supposed to be on your way to New York.'

'We turned around as soon as we heard. I can't believe this has happened. Who could have done this to Ariana? She's just a child.' Sarah started to sob as Alice held her.

'Do they know anything yet?' Jon asked, turning to Emily.

'Not that I've heard. They're doing tons of interviews. Here, over on Manchebo Beach, and Ariana's friends. It's a huge undertaking, I think. I haven't seen Annie or Martin and I'm waiting to see Thomas.'

'I used to babysit her,' Sarah said, her voice strained. 'She was so sweet, always. I remember when she was young, six or seven, she wanted me to fix her hair like mine – braids, a ponytail. Or, if I arrived wearing shorts and she had a skirt on or long pants, she would make her mother change her outfit. She loved to draw and write stories.' She started crying again. 'I can't believe this. How could this have happened?'

'There, there, honey,' Alice said. 'You

should head up to the house – your mom and dad are up there.'

Sarah wiped her eyes. 'Well, it won't do going up there like this. I'm sure Mom's a mess. She and Kat are such good friends. Just give me a minute to settle myself,' she said, as Jon put his arm around her.

'I'd walk up with you, dear, but I'm waiting to be interviewed. I shouldn't be long. You head up, though. I'm sure it would help your mother.'

'You're right,' she said, noticing Emily for the first time. 'Oh, Emily ... isn't this just awful. I guess Thomas—'

'It is, and Thomas is totally swamped. I know he feels incredible pressure to find out who did this. Such a beautiful young girl. I'm waiting to talk to him.'

Just then Penny came to the door. 'Alice?'

'Yes, coming, Penny,' she said, heading inside. 'Oh and Sarah, your Aunt Joanne is inside being interviewed.'

Sarah just rolled her eyes as she and Jon headed up to the house.

Emily sat back down and turned again to watch the water. The bay beach was calm, like glass. Small ripples lapped the shore and Emily felt almost mesmerized as she watched. Once again, her thoughts turned to the bracelet. She remembered Michael's words as she had tried to give it back to him, 'No, Emily, it's yours. Please, keep it. Keep it as a reminder of better days.' What could have happened to it? She couldn't believe that Ariana had taken it, but then someone else must have – taken it and given it to her?

'Emily.' Thomas was heading towards her. He put his arms around her and drew her to him. 'I'm sorry; this isn't the way I wanted these few days to be. There's nothing—'

'Thomas, please, you have a job to do, an incredibly important job. Did you want to inter—'

'No, I was just coming out to say I have to leave. I'm heading back up to the Van Meeterens'. They're ready to ID the body. I thought maybe just Christiaan would do it, but Kat's insisting. She wants to see her. I know how devastating this will be. I wish ... They've had a few hours to absorb the first shock, although, God help them, it will get worse. They also want to talk to me. It seems they've been thinking and, well...'

Emily looked closely at him. The strain of the last few hours was clearly evident – his face seemed lined and pale, and there was dark stubble on his cheeks and chin. 'Go, I'll be here when you get back. And please, don't put too much pressure on yourself. You're not the only one working on this.'

For just a moment, his eyes became hard. 'This one is mine to solve.'

SIXTEEN

He noticed the guard at the gate as soon as he drove up. Security, not police, he thought. Good. He checked the rear-view mirror. No one behind him. That was good too. He was hoping not to meet anyone he knew.

'Afternoon,' the guard said, peering into the car. 'Are you a guest at the Bluffs?'

'Me, I only wish,' he said with a smile. 'No, I'm here to see a Detective Keary.'

'Name?'

'William Dunlop,' he said as the guard looked at his clipboard. 'I have a four o'clock appointment.'

'Right. Sorry, can I see some ID?'

Billy fished out his wallet and took out his driver's license.

'Thanks,' the guard said, looking at it. 'You can park to the right side of the main house. Reception is just inside the door. Someone there will help you.'

Billy nodded and headed through the

gates. When he reached Reception a young, pretty girl behind the desk greeted him with a wide smile.

'I'm William Dunlop. Actually, call me Billy. All my friends do,' he said with a slightly suggestive smile. 'I have a four o'clock appointment with a Detective Keary.'

'Yes, William,' she said – no smile this time. 'Please take a seat. He should be with you shortly.'

Billy sat down trying to look serious, even concerned. He shouldn't have made that friends comment. He should have realized that no one here would be in a joking mood today. He'd have to do better with Keary. He picked up a magazine, browsing through it while he waited and checked out the room – two other young guys, obviously day staff, one looked kind of familiar; an older man dressed in khaki shorts and a light blue shirt, probably a guest; and a middle-aged woman, light grey uniform, white apron, a chambermaid. Then he looked out to the terrace.

This is more interesting, he thought. That's the redhead; wonder if she's waiting to be interviewed. He tried to catch her name but couldn't. And the other two, he recognized them – the bride and groom. She was bawling and there was an older woman hugging her. He didn't know who the woman was but she looked like family.

Then the girl from Reception headed out there. She called the older woman Alice and they both walked back in and headed for an office door behind the desk. The bride and groom left the terrace and the redhead sat back down and stared at the beach. Not much more to see there.

Billy was getting impatient, and as he sat waiting he got increasingly jittery. Should have thrown a couple of pills into my pocket, he thought. He started twisting his hands and brushing his fingers through his hair. His lip twitched a little and he rubbed his mouth to stop it. This won't do, he thought, and got up and walked over to the desk to give himself something to do.

'Any idea how long this will be?' he asked the girl, then thought better of it. 'It's OK, I don't mind waiting. It's just that I got a gig at six, have to be there at five thirty, and if I'm gonna be late I wanna let the boss know.'

'I'm sorry,' she said, a little friendlier this time. 'They're running a little late and...'

A tall, good-looking man in a somewhat rumpled suit entered the reception room and quickly walked out onto the terrace. Billy recognized him right away. The guy from the news conference, heading the investigation. Moller, that was his name. He immediately went over to the redhead. Emily, he called her, and put his arms around her. Billy didn't like this. These two are more than friends, he thought. Damn, one more friggin' complication.

Just then the girl at the desk called his name. Uh oh, it's time. Better be sharp.

He entered the room easily, willing himself to walk slowly and smile as he said, 'Detective Keary, I'm William Dunlop.' He didn't do the Billy routine this time.

'Have a seat,' Keary said, looking at a file in front of him. 'I'm sure you're aware of what happened this morning on Manchebo Beach?'

'Yeah ... I am, sir,' Billy answered, switching to his most sincere voice. 'Awful, awful thing.'

'You also probably know that the girl was last seen here on Saturday night. We're talking to anyone who might have seen her.'

'I hadn't heard that. Wow, that's tough for the Bluffs. But I'm afraid I can't really help you. See, I was working set-up here on Friday from nine to seven. It was a pretty long day.'

'Why don't you tell me a little bit about

yourself, William, or is it Billy?'

'Billy, my friends call me Billy. Well, I was born in the States—'

'Where 'bouts?'

'New York, well, upstate New York, a little town called Athens, right on the Hudson River.' A dump of a town – three thousand people, a few stores, a couple of restaurants and a shitload of old houses people liked to call historic. Billy hated it. His father worked odd jobs and his mother minded the kids and occasionally cleaned other people's houses.

'How'd you end up down here?'

'After I graduated from high school I tried college. I was smart enough, but it just wasn't for me. So I picked up and moved to New York City.' He should've said he'd barely graduated from high school after three suspensions in his senior year. And the college thing? That was his mother's fantasy. He was smart enough, all right – smart enough to get out of that town as soon as he could.

'I had done a couple of summers as a waiter at home, so I looked for a wait job in the city. I couch-surfed for a while and then got a place in Brooklyn with three other guys.' Actually, he'd lived pretty rough in the city. He was a busboy and he worked in a coffee shop until a guy he met got him in as relief bartender in a lower eastside dive.

'The girl's name was Ariana Van Meeterens. Does that name mean anything to you?'

Whoa, Billy was thrown by the change of subject. It took him a minute to answer. 'Sorry, no, not a name I recognize. But if she was a guest here I probably—'

'She wasn't a guest. She was actually working, babysitting.'

'Well, as I said, I wasn't here on Saturday, just Friday.'

'So, in New York, you're working in this restaurant – was it a restaurant?'

'No, after that I got a job as a bartender.' Better stick close to the truth. 'That's how I ended up here in Aruba. A friend of mine had a friend who had worked down here tending bar. He told me about it and I was sold. Always hated the winters, the cold and the snow, so I used my savings and headed down.' Well, he didn't have any savings, but he beat it out on his last month's rent and that was enough for a plane ticket.

'How long ago was that?'

'Wow, that's gotta be almost three years ago.'

'And, what have you been doing in Aruba since then?'

'Mostly bartending. I was working down in San Nicolas but I quit a couple of weeks ago. Didn't like the way my employer treated customers. You know, switching out the booze, no buy backs. That's why I've been picking up some day jobs like I did here at the Bluffs. A friend of mine told me they were doing some day hires and I always loved the Bluffs – it's a great resort. I make enough to get by and I love the island. I know I can't do that forever and, sooner or later, I'm going to have to think about the future, but for now...' Actually, he had been thinking a lot about his future and had made a pretty sweet plan until that stupid bitch had screwed it up.

'And what was your friend's name?'

Billy was ready for this. 'Joey ... uh, Joseph Salter.' Although Joey hadn't exactly told him about the day job. It was more like Billy had asked him, but who cares?

Keary picked up a picture and handed it to Billy. 'Recognize her?'

Again, the switch. Billy knew this was a tricky moment. He looked down at the picture. She was really something, he thought. Stupid bitch. 'Man, she's really pretty,' he said, not lifting his eyes from the picture as if studying it carefully, and giving himself a

144

minute before he faced the detective. 'I don't get it, how could someone do something like that?'

'Did you, by any chance, see her at all on Friday?'

'On Friday?' Billy repeated, trying to act surprised. 'Nah. No way, I would have remembered her ... Was she here on Friday?'

Keary didn't answer that. Instead, he asked Billy to describe the work he had done on Friday. He wanted a lot of details – what time he arrived, where he worked, with whom, what did he do on his breaks, did he work on his own at all, was he down near the bay beach, did he have access to any of the guests' rooms, what time did he finish, what did he do afterward ... Billy was patient, careful. He answered all the questions, even when they were repeated and asked in different ways, even when he felt himself wanting to scream, *You stupid bastard, you think I'm brainless. I'm smarter than you, than all of you.* It was pretty easy, actually. He could answer everything. Nothing to hide, just that few minutes, three, maybe five, on Friday evening when he'd met up with Ariana on the path. That had been stupid, careless. She'd had that baby with her and the baby had started crying so he'd left pretty quickly.

He'd known it was risky, but he had to talk to her, arrange to pick her up at the end of the night, and he was pretty sure no one had seen him. Pretty sure – was that good enough?

The interview went on for half an hour and Billy felt that he couldn't take much more. He tried to stay as steady as he could but felt his fingers starting to move almost uncontrollably and he knew he was licking his lips too often. Luckily, it looked like Keary was starting to wind it down.

'Last question: where were you last night?'

Billy was careful. 'Let's see. I went to the beach, stayed pretty late. Went home and crashed for a couple of hours. Too much sun. When I got up I was starving so I headed out to Big Mama's. Nothing better than their curry grouper.' OK, stop talking so much, keep it simple. 'I hung out with friends and then headed over to Charlie's. I know it can be a little touristy, especially on Saturday nights, but it was late and usually it's a local crowd by then. Did some shots and then left there, late, probably 'bout two.'

'OK, Billy. Thanks for coming in,' Keary said. Then, the usual send-off stuff – we may need to talk with you again; if you think of anything, anything at all, here's my card.

And then, 'Oh, Billy, can I see your driver's license?'

Billy handed it over and Keary made a copy. 'For our records,' was all he said as he handed it back.

Billy walked out as casually as he'd walked in. He would have loved to talk up the girl at the desk but he didn't dare. Best not to be too memorable around here, just be one more working stiff. As he walked out the door, he heard the girl at the desk say to the redhead, 'Emily, Annie was wondering if you'd like to stop by the house.'

He was going to have to do something about her, he thought. But not now. Now he needed something to calm his nerves and those pills in the car weren't going to do it. He'd head over to the alley near Senor Frogs; he was sure he could score what he needed there.

SEVENTEEN

Emily walked up the path to Martin and Annie's villa. It stood just beyond the main house on the bluff overlooking the ocean. She paused for a minute to appreciate Annie's gardens, so lush with flowers that they almost looked like a painter's palette. The house was closely built into the rocks and scrub, so much so that you almost didn't notice it from the rest of the resort. Emily knew from last year that the views were spectacular and the wide veranda that ran the length of the house managed to catch both sunrise and sunset.

She tapped on the front door and heard Annie call from the living room, 'We're in here, Emily.'

The house was as beautiful as she remembered it. Like the rest of the resort, it was almost all white except for the dark wood and splashes of bright tropical color. A series of French doors opened onto the veranda and one could watch the ocean from almost anywhere in the room. The artwork on the walls was local, but different from the works in the guest rooms down below. Here the canvasses were enormous and vibrant, dominating the room. There were just four of them, hung on the wall opposite the French doors.

Emily had asked Martin about them last year. A very talented young artist was behind them, Martin had told her. Poor, with little formal training, abandoned when he was quite young by a single mother who couldn't break a devastating drug habit. He had been raised at the Imeldahof's Children's Home in Noord. After that he had struggled for a time, lived here and there, got involved in drugs himself. But a friend of Martin and Annie's had seen some of his small, primitive works and reached out to him. A talented artist herself, she believed that he had a real gift. At her urging, Martin had sponsored him, eventually providing a small living space, which had once been a gardener's cottage on the property, and helped to promote his work on the island. He gained some success and was seen as one of Aruba's up-and-coming artists, but his chaotic early life had left his health fragile and he died very young.

These were the last four paintings that he did, a gift to Annie and Martin.

Annie looked better than she had earlier. She sat on the couch, Sarah on one side of her and Alex on the other. Martin and Jon stood talking quietly near the door to the veranda.

'How are you, Annie?' Emily asked with concern.

'I'm better. I spoke with Kat a while ago. She sounds terrible, but is no longer angry with Thomas and me. They're so shattered and the afternoon has been horrific, questioning everything, questioning themselves. Could someone Ariana knew have done this? Was there something they should have done? Something they should have known? Something they missed?' Her voice shook a little. 'But they both realize that their help is needed if the police are going to find whoever did this. Their older girls are both home, distraught, of course. They were very close. It's … it's heartbreaking.'

'I'm sure they're all devastated.'

'Kat said Thomas was on his way over there, so I thought you might want to join us here for dinner.'

'Thank you, Annie, but I'm fine really. If all of you want to be alone, I—'

'No, no, it's better to have some company. We can't really face going down below, although I feel terrible abandoning all our guests. But not tonight; I can't face it tonight. Tomorrow, perhaps.' For a moment, Annie turned and looked out at the water. Alex reached out and took her mother's hand. 'I invited Peggy to join us, and Maggie. I'm sure Peggy doesn't want to talk to anyone and now that everyone knows, well, there are always a few who would bother her.' She shook her head and looked intensely at Emily. 'Maybe it's natural, but I find it so intolerable. What's wrong with people, being drawn to something as tragic as this, like it's a reality show.'

'It's hard to understand, but I've seen it before,' Emily said, remembering the times in her old job when she would be dealing with some dreadful event – a young man threatening suicide on a bridge, a young woman attacked in a building stairwell, a child shot on the playground in the midst of a gang war. People crowding around, gawking, holding up cell phones to snap a picture.

'Martin's sister Alice will join us and ... well ... possibly his sister-in-law.'

'I've met both of them,' Emily said. 'Alice seems lovely.'

In no time, the living room was busy. Alice had just finished her interview and seemed spent. 'Aunt Alice,' Alex said, getting up from the couch. 'Come sit here next to Mom.'

Martin was at Alice's side right away. 'Alice, have this,' he said, handing her a glass of white wine.

'A man after my own heart.' Alice took a long gulp. 'How are you, Annie?'

'Better, thanks, Alice, although heartsick. How'd your interview go?'

'Short. I hadn't seen Ariana at all. Didn't even realize she was here until Kat told me at the wedding. How is she ... and Christiaan?'

'They're devastated, how else could they be? The girls are home, thank God. I spoke to Kat a short while ago. The police are there now. It's been a grueling day. I told her I would come by in the morning.'

'Where's Christopher?' Alice asked, looking around the room. Christopher was Annie's younger brother. An art collector and dealer, he lived in Paris with his partner, Henri. Emily had met him at the wedding – tall and slim, like Annie, and the same salt and pepper hair, although his had decidedly more pepper. He was strikingly good looking, as was his partner. She and Thomas had a long conversation with them about the Paris art scene, something Emily knew little about, but to her surprise, a subject Thomas had a real interest in.

'He'll be up shortly. He had some calls to make. You know, with the time difference, it's midday in Paris and work—'

'Oh, you don't have to tell me; Joe's been on his cell phone all day. I know they say that these devices make our lives easier, more connected, but I don't know. It seems you just can never really get away.'

Joe, Alice's husband, followed her into the room. 'What can I get you, Joe?'

'I would love a Scotch, Martin. Any kind and—'

'I know,' Martin said, holding up his fingers, 'with just two ice cubes.'

Peggy and Maggie arrived next. Emily was surprised at how tired and drawn Peggy looked. 'I'm afraid no nap for either of us,' she said as she sat, Maggie on her knee. 'She's usually a great napper but she just couldn't settle down.' Maggie pulled at Peggy's short brown curls, giggling as she watched them spring back.

'Why don't I take her for a little while?' Alex said, reaching down to pick her up. 'I haven't seen her in weeks. We'll head into the den to play. You relax for a bit, have a glass of wine.'

Emily wandered into the den after them. In the corner the TV played silently. She watched as the images flashed across the screen. The memorial on the beach had grown massive – flowers and notes, stuffed animals, snapshots, candles. The TV cameras scanned back and forth, zeroing in on particularly poignant scenes – a young man attaching a picture of Ariana sailing to a wreath of flowers, his mother standing behind him; two girls crying as they left a note and a pink teddy bear; a pinwheel twirling slowly in the breeze; a sign, *We'll never forget you*. Emily was glad she couldn't hear the reporter's voice.

Dinner was a quiet affair, at least until Martin's sister-in-law, Joanne, arrived. 'Martin, Annie,' she exclaimed as she entered the front door. 'This has been the worst experience. Martin, how could you do this? Sitting around with all those people waiting for that policeman. And then, all those questions. I just cannot understand it.'

'The police had to interview everyone, Joanne. I'm sorry if it disturbed you,' Martin said solicitously, but the look on Annie's face conveyed a very different message.

'Well, of course it was disturbing. The whole thing was disturbing and you know with my blood pressure, well, this—'

'Joanne, why don't you come and sit down?' Martin pulled out a chair at the end of the table, far away from Annie and, unfortunately for Alice, right next to her.

'Yes, Joanne, come and sit with me. You can tell me all about it,' Alice said with a roll of her eyes that Joanne didn't even notice.

But Joanne was not content sharing with just Alice and, as soon as she sat down, she commanded the attention of the whole table. 'I told that young man everything I knew. I saw that girl yesterday – no, Friday – and I'm sure I saw someone with her. Not that baby.' Joanne had not even noticed that Maggie was seated in a high chair near the other end of the table. 'How could I have missed them? The baby was crying. I thought you didn't allow young children at the Bluffs, Martin?'

'Aunt Joanne,' Sarah interrupted, an edge to her voice, 'Peggy,' she pointed down the table, 'is a good friend from New York. You must remember; she was at the wedding. And Maggie,' she pointed again, 'is her daughter.'

'Oh, yes, yes, that's the baby,' Joanne said with a short wave of her hand. Emily was amazed at how Joanne kept going, totally unaware of the expressions on the faces of those around the table. My God, she's clueless, Emily thought.

'Well, I'm sure that there was someone with her. It was almost dark, but I think it was a young man.'

'Did you recognize him, Joanne?' Annie said, now totally absorbed in what Joanne was saying. 'Do you know what he looked like? Could you recognize him again?'

'Oh, Annie, you know my eyes. Just a couple of months ago Doctor Greenberg wanted to do surgery. I just couldn't face it. Do you know that they do that operation with your eyes open? I thought about it. I imagine it would be a great help, and Doctor Greenberg said—'

'Joanne, please,' Martin interrupted her. 'This could be terribly important. Could you give the police a description?'

'I was just trying to explain, Martin,' Joanne said with a huff. 'About my eyes and what Doctor Green—'

'Enough with your eyes, Joanne,' Alice said, banging her hand on the table. 'Could you just answer Martin's question? Could you give the police a description?'

'Well, no, of course not,' Joanne said, obviously annoyed about the lack of interest in her eyes. 'Oh, but that didn't stop them from asking a million questions. Where were they? Were they near any of the guest rooms, the ones at the end of the bay beach?'

'Did you happen to notice what the young man was wearing?' Peggy asked.

'Wearing?' Joanne said, as if offended. 'Well, he was dressed like all the rest of them. Pants and a shirt, light colors, but I couldn't really tell what they were – as I said, my—'

'Why do you ask, Peggy?' Annie asked before Joanne could mention her eyes again.

'Oh, I'm sure it's nothing.' Peggy looked thoughtful for a moment. 'Just, I saw this young guy on the path. He looked sort of familiar so I figured he was staff, but there was something—'

'Well, I didn't see them near the bay beach,' Joanne said, not wanting to lose the spotlight. 'I asked this policeman why, what did the bay beach have to do with this and he said something about a missing gold bracelet. Don't ask me what that's all about, but they seemed mighty interested in it.'

Annie looked at Martin and then at Emily.

'Joanne, my father had that eye surgery,' Emily said, wanting to change the subject.

'Really, my dear, and how...' Joanne immediately engaged Emily in a discussion about her father's operation, tuning out the rest of the conversation at the table, but in the background Emily could hear Sarah and Alice's questioning about the bracelet and Annie's response: 'I think it's best if we leave that until later.'

The rest of the dinner was eaten in relative quiet. There was great disappointment on both Annie and Martin's faces with Joanne's answer. You could see how much they had hoped that this might be a break in the case. There was also a noticeable frustration with Joanne and her self-centered chatter. Alice could barely acknowledge her, but Joanne was oblivious.

'Alice,' she said towards the end of dinner, 'I thought I'd go into Oranjestad tomorrow. I can't bear how dreary it is here. Why don't you join me? We can go to your shop, Sarah.'

'I don't think I'll be opening tomorrow, Aunt Joanne. Most of my regulars expect me to be away and I think I'll take the time.'

'And I promised Joe we would spend the day at the beach,' Alice said.

'Really, well, it looks like I'll be on my own.

Martin, would you have Nelson drive me?'

'I don't think I can spare Nelson tomorrow, Joanne. We're opening up the dining room and with all that's happened there's a great deal—'

'That's fine,' Joanne said in a huff. 'I'll call a taxi.'

'You don't have to do that, Joanne. I'll ask Penny to arrange one for you. I'm sorry...'

But Joanne had stopped listening.

Beyond that, everyone seemed emotionally unable to talk about the events of the day and it didn't seem as if any other topic was quite worthy of being discussed. People ate in a desultory manner, hardly tasting the food and keeping their eyes mostly on the table. Sarah asked about a few of the wedding guests and Annie talked to Martin a bit about plans for the next day, but the only real relief was provided by Maggie who gurgled and smiled, playing clap hands with her mother and peek-a-boo with Sarah. Emily was greatly relieved when the phone rang. Martin spoke quietly for a few minutes and then said, 'It's for you, Emily. It's Thomas.'

EIGHTEEN

Emily quickly said her goodnights to the group as she headed out to meet Thomas. Peggy and Maggie left with her – it was easy to see that they were both exhausted. 'Eight o'clock is beyond her bedtime,' Peggy said. 'And with no nap. Maybe she'll sleep late in the morning.'

It was dark as they walked down the path to the main house. The light in Reception was the only one on. The interviews must be over, Emily thought. She could see Penny sitting working at her desk. It was strange to see the darkened dining room and the lights on the terraces turned off – usually their glow would illuminate the path. Dinner was available at the beach bar, but it was a quiet affair with no steel band or flaming torch-lights in the sand. A few people lingered over coffee, but for the most part the resort seem-ed almost empty.

'Did Thomas say how the afternoon had

gone?' Peggy asked.

Emily shook her head. 'We didn't really talk. I think he had just left Kat and Christiaan's. He went with them to ID the body.' Even the thought of that made Emily shudder. 'He sounds exhausted. He had one more call to make, to the chief, I think, and then he was heading over here. I'm going to meet him at the gate.'

Emily noticed how dark the path down to their rooms by the bay beach was. She had never noticed that before. Were some of the lights out, she wondered, or perhaps it was just the lack of light in the dining room? 'I have time,' she said. 'I could walk down with you.'

'No, you don't need to bother,' Peggy answered. 'Martin gave me this penlight to make my way.' She flashed its small beam ahead of her. It made a bright but narrow circle. 'And once I get down there, the suite's outside lights should be on. Maybe the darkness will put Maggie to sleep. She's already in her pyjamas. Then I could just lift her into her crib.' She paused. 'I asked Thomas about Maggie and me leaving. He said he hoped we wouldn't, not just yet. I told him how Ted felt, that he wanted us home. He said he didn't know if he could force us to stay, but could we at least give him one more day.'

'What will you do?'

'I don't know … I'll decide tomorrow. I like Thomas, Emily. I know this isn't the time to be thinking about this, but I hope things work out for the two of you.'

'Thanks, Peggy,' Emily said. 'I should go; he's probably out there by now.'

Neither of them noticed the figure who stood listening in the shadows of a nearby shed. Wearing black pants and a black long-sleeved shirt, he was almost invisible. His eyes were alert and intense as he watched them standing at the fork.

That makes my choice a lot easier, he thought as he watched them part. He would follow the one with the baby. He made his way slowly, his feet barely touching the ground. He stayed close to the bushes, skirting the bar where people sat. He was careful not to rustle the leaves of the plants or step on fallen twigs. The night was eerily quiet. He stayed a short distance behind, keeping her in his sight. He needed to know which room was hers – just in case.

The path leading to the front gate was also

dark and Emily turned back to check how Peggy and Maggie were doing. She couldn't see them at all – even the beam of light had been swallowed up by the night. Heavy clouds shrouded the moon and somewhere a dog howled. Emily shivered in spite of the warmth of the night.

Thomas was waiting by the gate, his car parked nearby. 'Emily,' he said, pulling her towards him. 'Oh, Emily.' He hugged her, and for a few minutes said nothing.

'I'm sure it was awful for you, Thomas.'

'It was, but you can't imagine what it was like for Christiaan and Katrien. Can we walk for a bit?'

As they headed down the path, Thomas talked, almost compulsively. 'Their child, so young and beautiful,' he said, his head shaking and bent. 'I will never get used to this. I don't know how these parents can do it.'

'They have no choice. They have to—'

'Yes, someone has to ID the body, but you can't understand what it's like.' Thomas' voice was strained, raspy. 'The initial shock is always devastating, but then it becomes this intimate moment – they want to touch her, to stroke her face and talk to her, to tell her how much they loved her ... to say good-bye.' Thomas shuddered.

Emily could feel the tears slipping down her face. She gripped his hand and held on tightly. They had reached the sea wall. 'Why don't we sit?'

Darkness surrounded them, but somehow that made talking easier. 'Do you know anything more, Thomas?'

'Not much. The interviews at Manchebo Beach have yielded nothing. No one heard anything; no one saw anything. We found the maintenance guy from the resort next door and the beach tennis players. Nothing. The CCTV cameras were pretty useless. Most of them are trained on the hotel and shop entrances, some on the parking lots. No one really monitors the beach and, even if they did, I don't think we'd find anything.'

'How did the interviews here go?'

'Pretty much the same. People saw Ariana – walking the baby, playing with her on the beach, but not much else. We're going to do some follow-up tomorrow. One person, Martin's sister-in-law, might have seen something, but—'

'I heard. She was at dinner. She said she saw a young man with Ariana, but then went on and on about her eyes not being good. I think Annie was ready to kill her—'

'She was the same with Detective Keary.

164

Couldn't get her to focus on the question or give a simple answer. We'll interview her again tomorrow.'

'At dinner, she did mention something about the bracelet.' Emily said this carefully, knowing what Thomas's reaction might be.

'What ... goddammit. I specifically said no mention of the bracelet. What in the hell ... Who did the interview?'

'I'm not sure. Didn't think to ask. But she didn't seem to have any idea what it was about so I doubt she'll say anything to anyone.'

'I'll find out more about it later. The team is meeting back at headquarters to review all the interviews.'

'What will you do next?'

'Well, the Van Meeterens talked a little about changes they'd seen in Ariana recently. Small stuff mostly. Breaking up with her boyfriend – nice kid, local. They went to school together. They said she used to be crazy about him, but then about a month ago she didn't want to see him anymore. Poor kid was heartbroken.'

Emily wondered if it was the young man she had seen on TV attaching the photo to the wreath. 'Nothing more painful than a teenage crush,' she said, but the poor boy was dealing with a lot more than that.

'I had to ask them if he was the jealous type. They looked shocked. Christiaan especially. They insisted no, but we'll have to interview him first thing in the morning. And then there's school itself. Ariana had always been a great student. Good grades, really involved. She was going to look at top-notch American colleges. But recently she seemed less interested in activities; her grades were slipping. They chalked it up to senior year. Their older girls had gone through it, but now they're not so sure.'

'It is something high-school seniors go through,' Emily said. 'I remember it with my sisters and brother. It would start in late October, when the thrill of being seniors wore off, and from then till March keeping them interested was like pulling teeth. I think a lot of it was the whole college application stuff – such pressure.'

'Well, tomorrow we'll start in-depth interviews with all her school friends. I'm not looking forward to it. It's hard with these kids. Some of them will be so upset, they can't even think let alone answer, and some won't want to say anything. Even if they feel it's something we should know, they feel they're betraying their friend.'

'Did she have friends outside school?'

'A couple but mostly school friends; a crowd she hung out with. Christiaan also said she had missed a couple of curfews recently. Not by much, but that wasn't like her. They went pretty light on it; it had happened with their older girls.'

'Was there any mention of the bracelet?'

'I didn't ask about it again; more important to keep them talking. But as I was leaving, Christiaan said, "About that bracelet – we've never seen it before."'

'We'll have to ask her friends about it, so you have to be ready, Emily. Once we do that, we know it will get out and we'd like to be the ones to put it out there. For now, we'll try to keep the inscription and your name out of it, but I'm not sure how long we can get away with that.'

'It doesn't matter, Thomas. The only thing that matters now is finding who did this.'

Thomas rubbed his eyes. 'I better get back. I'm sure the others will be there and we have a lot of interviews to go over. I'll walk you back to your room.'

'You don't have to do that. I'm fine. You should go.'

'No, I'd like to – it's so dark. Martin should put more lights along this path. And anyway, this will give me a couple more minutes before I have to face...' His voice trailed off.

'Oh, Thomas, I almost forgot. Peggy mentioned something at dinner about seeing a young man on the path on Friday when she was heading to rehearsal. He wasn't with Ariana, but she said there was something about him—'

'OK,' he answered but his voice sounded dispirited. 'I'll have someone talk to her in the morning.'

They walked quietly along the path. It did seem darker than usual, Emily thought, and the outside lights to her and Peggy's suites were out. She considered saying something to Thomas but knew it would only delay him. 'Goodnight, Thomas. Try to get some sleep. Tomorrow—'

'I know,' he said, kissing her lightly on the lips. 'Goodnight, Emily.' And he turned and walked back up the path.

It was only as Emily turned on the inside light that she noticed the shattered glass on the doorstep.

NINETEEN

Monday morning dawned, brutally hot. Thomas arrived at headquarters at six-thirty, and didn't know why he had even bothered to go home. The desk sergeant was waiting, his face glum.

'That bad?' Thomas enquired as he picked up the stack of morning papers. 'Is everyone inside?'

'All there. Should I hold any calls?'

'Please,' Thomas answered, opening the conference room door.

They sat around the table poring over the papers. The headlines were as gruesome as they imagined they would be – 'Beauty on the Beach', 'Washed Up.' One of the papers made reference to the island's previous cases with a glaring 'Not Again,' and even the more staid headline, 'Body Washes Ashore on Manchebo Beach' appeared in one-inch type. Most of them featured a picture of Ariana; in one she was in a bathing suit.

Thomas groaned, looking at them and imaging the Van Meeterens' anguish this morning. Hopefully they wouldn't see the papers, but they'd be hard to miss. 'OK, everyone take one and comb through those stories. See if there's anything in there that we've missed. Any name mentioned that we don't have. Any detail we've overlooked. See if there's any creep who's come out from under a rock for a little publicity.'

He grabbed the top one and opened to page two. 'What the hell!' he screamed, holding the paper up to his men. There, in color, was a picture of Ariana's body lying on the beach. 'How the hell did this happen?' He slammed his hand down on the table. 'I said no pictures.'

His men just stared blankly back. 'It's not one of ours,' Hendricks said after a minute. 'It must have been someone with a cell phone or a long lens camera from the Bucuti resort.'

Thomas glared at him.

'Look, Chief, you know it's almost impossible to stop that these days.'

'You call them. Find out where the hell they got this picture. Put some pressure on. I want answers – now.'

Hendricks shook his head as the rest of

them turned back to the newspapers.

'Anything?' Thomas asked.

'There's a quote here from some guy who says he saw a guy and girl arguing over by Palm Beach, and another who saw the same thing on Eagle,' Millard said. 'Want me to check 'em out?'

'Yep. I want everything checked.'

'Uh oh,' Keary said. 'There's someone here who says he saw Ariana at Charlie's late on Saturday night. He gives a description of her doing shots. Another one, a girl, says she saw her outside.'

'Oh, come on.' Thomas threw down the paper he was reading. 'Why don't we have that? How is it that the newspapers are printing that stuff and we don't have it? Check with the desk and see if any of those calls that came in were about Charlie's. Have all those calls been followed up?'

Keary could almost see the veins popping in Thomas's neck. 'Not all of them. I'll check what hasn't been done.'

He left the room and returned a minute later. 'Sorry, Chief,' he said, coming back into the room. 'One was about a sighting at Charlie's but it came in late last night.'

'I don't give a damn how late it came in. I said I wanted everything, *everything* followed up, and not a day later. We can't afford this. Get on it.'

Thomas tried to calm down; he knew barking at everyone wasn't going to help. 'OK, let's draw up a plan for the day. Keary, you check on those leads at Charlie's, track those people down and find out what they saw. And Hendricks, don't bother trying to go after the newspaper for that picture. They won't tell you anyway. No sense wasting our time.' Thomas could sense the decrease in tension in the room. 'Keary, you head over to San Nicolas. Check out the other places on the street. If she really was in the area, we want to know about it.'

'Right, Chief,' Keary responded.

'Hendricks, we'll start on the list of kids. I'll take the boyfriend first. Andrew Marsden.' He looked down at the list. 'You take the two girls who were her best friends, Ashruf and de Veer. Is Turner at the Van Meeterens'?'

'She is, been there since six,' Hendricks answered, heading out the door.

Thomas called Grace Turner as he drove. 'Everything quiet there?'

'So far, just one truck and a couple of cars, but that won't last long.' Grace was a top detective. On the force for a little over five years, she was smart and proactive but also intuitive and caring. On top of that, she was a knock-out and that made her perfect for undercover work. With her face and figure nobody would suspect her of being a cop. Thomas had relied on her in a lot of difficult spots and she had always come through.

'OK, just make sure they don't get too close.'

He pulled up in front of the Marsdens – a pleasant house with a small front garden, a wide porch and bright blue shutters, modest compared to the Van Meeterens'. A middle-aged woman sat on the porch looking at the morning paper. 'Mrs Marsden?' Thomas asked, extending his hand. 'Chief Inspector Thomas Moller.'

'I've been expecting you, Inspector.' She put down the newspaper. 'I didn't want to read it inside. Andrew is so upset,' she said, wringing her hands. 'I imagine you're here to talk to him?'

'We have some questions. We know he was Ariana's boyfriend.'

'He's a good boy, Inspector. He was crazy about her. I don't know how much he can tell you; she broke up with him a few weeks ago. He's been moping around ever since. Come inside, please.'

Andrew Marsden was sitting on the couch, staring at the TV. His mother immediately went over and turned it off. 'Andrew, don't,' she said. 'This is Inspector Moller. He'd like to ask you a few questions.'

Andrew stood up and held out his hand. He was tall and good looking, with dark hair and a face that still bore traces of teenage acne. He stammered as he spoke. 'Inspector, I ... I ... don't know what I can tell you. Ariana and I haven't seen much of each other in the last couple of weeks, just a little at school.'

'Please, sit down,' Andrew's mother said to both of them. 'I'll make some coffee, Inspector.' Thomas would have said no, but he knew it would give her something to do and him a chance to talk to Andrew alone.

'How long were you and Ariana going out?' he asked.

'About six months,' Andrew said, his voice shaky. 'We started dating just before junior prom last year.'

'And you got along well?'

His eyes welled with tears and he nodded.

'And you broke up a few weeks ago?'

He nodded again.

'Can you tell me what happened?'

'Ariana broke up with me. I don't even

know why. Things had been going great, like always and then something just happened. At first, she said she was busy, you know, with school stuff—'

'When was that?'

'It was around the end of October. At first I thought, OK. A paper, an exam. She always worked real hard at school. But then about a week later she seemed to distance herself from me, actually from all of us. You know, usually we'd all hang out together on Friday nights, but she stopped coming. She'd still hang out with Olivia and Zoe sometimes, but not when I was around. Then she stopped picking up her cell when I called and started avoiding me at school. I knew it was over.'

'What did you think was going on?'

'I figured there was someone else. She was so pretty and such fun to be with.' The tears spilled over his eyes. He wiped them away. 'Sorry.'

'Was it someone at school?'

'I don't think so. I would have known. No, I don't have any idea who it was. I hardly saw her anymore. I tried once or twice to talk to her about it, but she just said, "Andy, please, I'm sorry but it's over."'

'Were you angry?'

'Angry? Yeah, I guess I was angry a little. But mostly I just couldn't understand. It happened so fast and there wasn't anything. No argument, no fight. I don't know.'

Thomas talked to Andrew for a while longer but didn't learn anything more. He asked about Ariana's habits, what she liked to do, who her friends were. Just as he was finishing up, his cell phone rang.

'Chief, it's Grace. I think you'd better get over here to the Van Meeterens'. Things are heating up and it's getting out of control.'

Thomas took only minutes to get there. There were five TV trucks out front, their motors running and lights on. A scrum of print reporters and a couple of photographers jostled nearby. And standing on the front lawn was an enraged Christiaan Van Meeterens'. Thomas could hear him screaming as he got out of the car.

'Get the hell out of here, all of you!' His face was purple with rage. 'What right do you have? This is my home, you have no right. God damn it ... Can't you see what you're doing to us?' His voice broke with anger. 'Moller,' he yelled, seeing Thomas. 'Get them the hell out of here.' And turning to the reporters, 'What is wrong with you, you vultures...'

Thomas could see the photographers moving forward and heard the whirring of the cameras. 'Get back,' he said, moving in front of Christiaan. 'All of you.' He practically charged them. 'Get back now.'

'Hey we have a right...' one of them called out.

'Don't tell me about your rights. In one minute you'll have the right to a jail cell. You've crossed the line and you know it. Now pull back.'

Grace moved forward, signaling for them to move, and they slowly started to set up further away from the house. 'Get a couple of uniforms up here, Grace,' Thomas said. 'And make sure they stay back.'

Thomas went up to Christiaan, whose anger had suddenly dissipated. 'Let's go inside, Christiaan,' he said quietly, placing his arm around him. 'Don't give them anything more.'

'They're nothing but parasites, scum, feeding off the tragedy of others,' Christiaan said as he sat down in the living room, his head in his hands. 'How could people ... The girls tried to go out earlier, just for a drive to get out of the house. They followed them, snapping their damn cameras, trying to get them to say something...' His voice dissolved into sobs.

Thomas waited. 'I'm sorry, Christiaan. You know we can do very little to stop them. We'll make sure they stay back but I can't get rid of them.'

'I know, I know. It's just—'

'How is Katrien?'

'Terrible. She's upstairs. She won't come down.'

'Can I go up?'

Christiaan nodded yes.

The yellow police tape that closed off Ariana's room had been ripped down. Inside Thomas found Katrien sitting on the floor, a suitcase at her side, its contents pulled out. Katrien held a pale blue sweater.

'She had already started packing for our trip,' she said, looking up at Thomas. 'She wasn't sure about this sweater. Was the color too light for winter in New York?' She put the sweater aside and picked up a soft, brown suede jacket. 'But she loved this. We bought it together two weeks ago. She said it was...' Katrien stroked the front, '...the softest...'

'Katrien, don't,' Thomas said, but he wasn't sure it was the right thing to say. How could anyone know what was? But Katrien appeared not to have even heard him.

'She was so excited. So looking forward to visiting the colleges. We had made so many plans – Williams, I think that was her first choice, but she wouldn't be sure until she saw the schools. Her sister is at Yale and she was thinking maybe that would be a good place. I wanted that, of course – the two of them together...'

Seeing Katrien surrounded by Ariana's clothes, holding them and stroking them, almost as if ... It was unbearably sad. 'Katrien, why don't you come downstairs?'

'Do you think that would have been a good thing?' A tear spilled slowly down her cheek. 'So strange. I worried about her going far away, like I did with her sisters. Would she be safe? She was looking at Columbia and I was a little nervous about the city ... you know. And now ... so strange.'

Thomas heard a noise behind him and was relieved to see Annie coming up the stairs. She said nothing, just went in and sat on the floor next to Katrien. 'Annie,' Katrien said, holding up the suede jacket, 'remember how much she loved this jacket.' Annie put her arms around her and Katrien wept. Thomas turned and headed downstairs.

The two girls, Ariana's sisters, sat on the couch with Christiaan, one of them holding his hand. 'How is she?' Christiaan asked.

'Annie is up there with her. I think that's good for now.'

Christiaan nodded.

When Thomas got outside things had quieted down. The uniforms were stationed at the end of the drive and the reporters and cameras had moved across the street. Grace stood to the side leaning against her squad car, arms folded, a look of pure murder on her face.

'Well, looks like they got the message,' Thomas said. 'I don't think you're needed here anymore. Let's let these guys handle it from here. I need you for more important things.'

Thomas headed back to headquarters, anxious now to get updates on Keary's and Hendricks' progress. If Ariana was at Charlie's, other people must have seen her and might know who she was with. It had been a Saturday night and the place would have been packed. He'd give the owner a call and see what kind of cooperation he would get. It was always tough in a situation like this. Bar owners loved publicity, but not this kind.

There was a TV crew and a number of reporters out front when he arrived. 'Chief

Inspector Moller, anything new on the Van Meeterens girl?' 'We've heard reports that she was at Charlie's bar on Saturday night. Is that true?' 'Have you interviewed the ex-boyfriend?'

Thomas avoided their questions. 'Nothing right now, fellas. We'll be having another press conference at twelve-thirty,' he said as they shouted at him.

'Messages,' he said to the desk sergeant.

'On your desk, sir. I sorted them, put what I thought was most important on top.'

Thomas rifled through them. The usual, mostly, except for two. One from Martin. 'Please call when you get this message. There's something I need to show you.' Thomas didn't like the sound of that. The other was from the owner of Charlie's. 'I think I need to talk to you ASAP.' Hmmm ... guess he's seen the morning papers, Thomas thought.

He turned on the TV in the corner, hoping to catch the noon updates when a breaking news story flashed on the screen. A woman's face appeared. She was leaning out of a taxi window right outside of the Bluffs, talking to a reporter. Thomas recognized her immediately – Martin's sister-in-law, Joanne Maitland.

'I told that young officer I saw someone with her, a young man, on Friday,' she was saying animatedly. 'I couldn't give them a description. I have bad eyes. But I'm not the only one who saw them.'

You could tell the reporter was excited to get this news. 'Can you tell us who else saw this young man?' he asked, pressing her for an answer.

'Well, the mother of that baby, the baby that she was minding.'

'Was that a guest here at the Bluffs for the wedding?'

'Yes, yes. Peggy something. She also saw the young man.'

'Can you tell us anything else? What's it like in there? Seems like they have this place pretty well sealed off.'

'Oh, they were doing lots of interviews yesterday, guests, staff. It was a madhouse. I had to wait almost an hour for my interview. Lots of questions and something about a gold bracelet.'

Thomas moaned, then cursed.

'What gold bracelet?' the reporter asked, practically jumping into the car.

'Well, I have no idea. I thought it was a strange question but that was it,' Joanne said as the reporter cut away.

'So, new information from the sister-in-law of Island Bluffs owner, Martin Maitland. As you just heard,' the reporter continued, 'it sounds like we have two witnesses and a mysterious gold bracelet. We're hoping to get more information on these developments in the murder investigation of Ariana Van Meeterens at the news conference now scheduled for twelve thirty. Meanwhile, in downtown San Nicolas...'

Thomas's phone started to ring almost immediately and the first call was from the commissioner.

'What the hell is going on?'

Thomas did his best to explain but the commissioner's parting words were ones he was thinking himself. 'I hope you're not losing control of this investigation, Thomas.'

TWENTY

Thomas spent the next hour trying to play catch-up. He met with Keary, Hendricks and Millard to go over the morning's interviews. Millard didn't think there was much to the two couples arguing on the beaches. The one on Palm was too early and the one on Eagle was the wrong hair color. Keary had a little more luck with the Charlie's guy. 'Sounded like Ariana had definitely been there, sometime after midnight,' he said.

'OK, you handle this message from the owner of Charlie's. Sounds like he might have some information for us. Millard, you head over with him. We need to know what he knows and who else was in that bar. I'm sure there were a ton of tourists – they might be hard to track down. We'll have to do an appeal on that. But I'm also sure there were lots of regulars – there always are. I want those names. Also, find out if Ariana was a regular.'

'Got it, Chief,' they both answered.

'Hendricks, what did you find out from the friends?'

'Well, the Ashruf girl,' he looked at his notes, 'Olivia ... Olivia Ashruf, didn't have much to say. They were good friends, did a lot of the same activities in school, studied together. She'd no idea who might have done this. Everyone loved Ariana – she was sweet and fun to be with. She didn't see her on Friday night or Saturday and knew she was babysitting on the weekend. They saw each other at school all the time and sometimes after. She knew the ex-boyfriend, Andrew Marsden – great kid. Didn't know why they broke up. They went out a couple of times on Friday and Saturday nights, especially after Ariana broke up with the boyfriend. She was vague about where they went. I think they had started going to some of the bars, but she didn't want to say. Bottom line – she's hiding something.'

'And the other one?'

'Zoe de Veer. A little more forthcoming. Basically, the same stuff as Ashruf, but said she hadn't seen as much of Ariana lately. I pressed a little, you know, new crowd, new boyfriend maybe? But she didn't seem to know anything. Still hung out with Ariana at school but not as much after. Said Ariana spent most of her time with Olivia and another girl, Liliana Florek. Gave me an address and phone number for her. I got the sense that she was a little put out that they weren't hanging out with her anymore. Said her parents were really strict so she couldn't go with them on Friday or Saturday nights. I asked her if she knew where they went. She said no but I think that's a lie ... Oh, and she said Ariana had dropped out of the school play.'

'OK,' Thomas said. 'I'm going to see if Turner can talk to the Van Meeterens again. I'll have her head back to the house and maybe she can talk to the sisters too. We have to find out a little more about what was going on with Ariana. They mentioned she had missed a couple of curfews recently – let's find out when exactly and if they know who she was supposed to be with. Then we can go back to these two girls. Hendricks, follow up on this Liliana Florek, see what she has to say.

'I have one call to make and then the press conference. I'm sure it will be a free for all, what with the statement from the sister-in-law and the news about the bracelet. I'm going to try to play that down. Bracelet found on her, trying to find out what we can about it – nothing about the inscription if we can help it. I don't like this talk of witnesses. None of that is firm. I'll head over to the Bluffs after to see what I can find out. Let's try to meet back here about three.'

Thomas put in a call to Martin. 'Thanks for getting back to me, Thomas,' Martin said, sounding worried. 'I need you to come to the Bluffs. There's something I need to show you.'

'No problem, Martin. I was going to head over there anyway. I need to talk to Peggy ... Martin, have you been watching the TV coverage?'

'No, we've been so busy trying to get some sense of normality back in here. Why, what's wrong, Thomas?'

'Your sister-in-law, Joanne, gave an interview to ATV—'

'Oh, dear God, no.'

'I'm holding a press conference in a few minutes but I'm sure they're replaying that over and over. Take a look; we can talk about it when I get there.'

'I'm so sorry, Thomas ... What can I say?'

The press conference was as harrowing as Thomas thought it would be. He tried his best to keep control of the room but without much success. His opening statement kept to the facts that they knew. Not much. Then Van Trigt gave a preliminary autopsy report. There were the usual questions about alcohol and drugs but it would take weeks for the toxicology screens to come back. The more painful were the ones about sexual assault. For once, Thomas appreciated Van Trigt's brusque demeanor. It didn't matter how many times the reporters asked the same question, he answered with the same brief response until they finally stopped asking.

When he returned to the mike to take questions the room erupted. Twenty hands flew into the air and as he called on one reporter, another would shout over him. They all had pieces of information – about San Nicolas and Charlie's bar, about the Bluffs, the witnesses and the gold bracelet, about who her friends were and where they usually hung out, and a ton of unfounded rumors – a boyfriend who assaulted her, a drug habit, even involvement in the red light district.

Thomas answered what he could as honestly as he could, but he held back the information about the inscription on the bracelet and Peggy's last name. He knew it wouldn't take long for them to find that out, but he hoped it would give him time to get out to the Bluffs, talk to Peggy and find out what else was going on there. He dispelled as many of the rumors as he could, but he knew his answers wouldn't stop them. Those rumors made good copy, even if they weren't true, and at this point, Thomas didn't even know what was true and what wasn't. He ended with a plea for anyone who was at Charlie's bar after midnight on Saturday night to contact the police. He knew this could be a nightmare, bring out all the hangers-on and crazies, but they had to talk to the people who were there. They had to find out if anyone saw Ariana with someone. As the last questions were thrown at him, he made a quick announcement that further updates would be provided late in the afternoon and left the room.

Several miles away, Billy Dunlop stared at his TV set. The bracelet, the goddamned bracelet. Why had he given it to her? What had he been thinking? So fuckin' stupid. He'd had it in his pocket on Saturday night – he hadn't been planning on giving it to her, he'd been planning on selling it. Hadn't even taken a good look at it. He should have been more careful but ... he knew how she'd be about it. How much it would mean to her. How she'd treasure it always. Wear it to the States ... for good luck. He'd needed her to want to do anything for him, and he just thought, hey, might as well give her this. Later, when the argument started, he'd forgotten all about it.

How had he gotten it so wrong? He'd thought for sure that she'd agree to his plan. She'd certainly fallen for him. Bu when he'd pushed the issue on Saturday night, she'd said no. Oh, she said she loved him all right, but she just couldn't do it. Stupid, naive girl. Said she could help him. Her father could find him a job. A job? What, bus boy at the Bluffs? Parking attendant at the mall?

No, he knew what the only way out was for him. It was too late. But he also knew a couple of big scores and he'd be home free. May make enough to buy himself a bar. He liked the thought of that.

But now this, and with a sinking feeling, he realized why the redhead and the kid's mother had looked familiar.

Could they trace it? he wondered. His hands started to sweat and he wiped his nose on his sleeve. His head itched and he raked his hands back and forth through his hair. If it was just a simple gold bangle it would be pretty hard to trace. They might be able to trace it to the States, maybe back to the maker or distributor, not much more. But now, he had witnesses. The older one had said she couldn't really see him – she had bad eyes. But the other one, the kid's mother ... The older one had said that the kid's mother had seen him. He couldn't believe she'd noticed him. She'd passed him so quickly on the path and he'd turned his head away. He started to pace around his small room. He was almost sure she was at the rehearsal before he met up with Ariana. Maybe he was overreacting. He had looked back a couple of times and seen her going down to where the chairs were set up on the beach.

What the fuck was he going to do? He'd have to do something about her. There wasn't anything he could do about the bracelet – too late for that – but the witness...

TWENTY-ONE

Thomas pulled up to the front gates and looked around. Three cars were parked further down the road, obviously press. The security guard approached his car.

'Are you a...' he said.

Thomas immediately flashed his badge.

'Oh, I'm sorry, Inspector Moller. I should have recognized you.'

'No problem,' Thomas answered. 'Those guys?' he continued, nodding at the cars.

'Reporters. They've been trying to get in here for the last two days, but they're real riled up now.'

'It's only going to get worse. I'll talk to Martin, see if we can give you a hand here. Is this the only entrance?'

'The only one people really see, but there are a couple of service entrances. I think Martin has staff covering those.'

'OK, I'll see what we can do.'

Thomas drove up to Reception and parked

around the back. He could see that the resort was busier today. The dining room was back up and running, lively with guests enjoying lunch. It looked vastly different from yesterday. The tables were dressed in sparkling white linens. Gone were the wilting birds of paradise, replaced with vases overflowing with neon hibiscus. Quiet conversation and gentle laughter filled the room. Thomas checked briefly to see if Emily might be there, but she wasn't. He headed to Reception and found Penny – also looking much brighter today – fielding guests' questions. In a way, it was hard to imagine that yesterday had even happened.

'Inspector Moller,' she said as soon as Thomas entered. 'I guess you're looking for Mr Maitland. Here, why don't you wait in the office and I'll find him for you.' She immediately opened the office door and ushered Thomas in.

'Thank you, Penny,' he said, thinking that she figured the guests seeing him might bring the mood down.

'Thomas,' Martin said as he entered. 'I'm so sorry. I saw the interview. I can't believe it. Joanne has always been ... Annie is furious. Wants me to tell Joanne to leave, but I don't think it would help. There's really no stopping her. How was the press conference?'

'What you'd expect. I tried to downplay the bracelet and I didn't give them Peggy's last name, but it will take them no time to find out and they'll be all over this place. We should talk about security.'

Martin sighed. 'I was trying to avoid having the police around ... the guests and all. But if you believe—'

'Let's think about it. Maybe it's not necessary, or we could use some plainclothes guys if—'

'Thomas, I'm so glad you're here,' Annie interrupted, coming in from the terraces. She looked drained. 'I just got back from Kat's...'

'How is she?'

'A little better, but do you know anything more?'

'Not much,' Thomas said. 'We do think Ariana was down in San Nicolas after she left here on Saturday night. We're sending a team to start doing interviews down there. It sounds like she may have been at Charlie's bar.'

'Charlie's? What would she have been doing there? Have you talked to her friends?'

'Some of them – her ex-boyfriend and a

couple of girlfriends. We've got a few more names but they haven't exactly been forthcoming. They think they're protecting Ariana. Too late for that. We'll push them a bit harder.'

'Kat talked a little more about the changes she'd seen in Ariana. Nothing big. A couple of broken curfews, less interest in school, a little more reticent than usual ... normal teenage stuff. But Christiaan also said that Ariana had been hanging out with a couple of new friends, girls he and Kat didn't really know that well. I could ask her for their names.'

'I'm heading over there after I leave here. If it's OK, I'll mention what you've told me.'

'Of course. There's nothing you can do about all those news vans and reporters outside their house?' Annie said. 'So disturbing.'

Thomas shook his head, reluctant to mention that those crews might well be outside the gates of the Bluffs once they got hold of Peggy's last name and the inscription on the bracelet. He'd have to warn Christiaan and Katrien about that, too. It was hard enough for them already, but once the newspapers got hold of it all, the speculation as to how Ariana had ended up with that bracelet would be devastating.

'Are Peggy and Emily around? I looked in the dining room but didn't see them,' Thomas said.

'They took Maggie to the Butterfly Farm,' Martin replied. 'They were anxious to get away for a little while. We thought it was a good idea. Nelson took them and ... I asked him to stay with them. They're on their way back, but this would be a good time to show you—'

'I'm sorry. I forgot you said there was something you needed me to see.'

'Let's head down to the suites on the bay beach. It's down there.'

A number of guests observed Thomas, Martin and Annie as they headed down. Thomas noticed the stares and more than a few whispered comments as people watched to see where they were going. Martin did his best to wave and smile at them. Nobody was fooled. Martin stopped at the door of Peggy's suite and Thomas immediately noticed the broken glass. 'What happened?'

Martin just pointed to Emily's door. 'The lights have been smashed. Both doors. We—'

'When?' Thomas asked with rising unease.

'Sometime last night, we believe. Peggy noticed the light was out, but she had a small flashlight with her so it was OK. She didn't notice the glass. Emily did.'

'But I was here with Emily last night,' Thomas said. 'We walked by the beach and then, well, I walked her almost to the door. I left her at the end of the path. Everything seemed fine. Martin, we're going to have to bring in a forensic team. I'm sorry. I know how difficult it will be to have this going on again.'

'No, no, Thomas. Please, whatever you need to do.'

'I don't want anyone else down here. Can you have Nelson bring Emily and Peggy straight to your house?'

'I'll call him right now,' Martin said.

'Thomas.' Annie's voice was full of concern. 'What do think is going on?'

'I don't know, Annie. But no one besides us knew about Peggy and Emily's connection to this case last night. They'll all know shortly, but last night? There's only one person who could have had any idea, and that person is the one who killed Ariana Van Meeterens.'

Annie and Martin looked stunned. No one said anything as they made their way back beyond Reception and up the path to Martin and Annie's house. Nelson was just pulling up and Emily quickly jumped out, anxious to see Thomas. Without hesitation she ran up and kissed him quickly on his lips. Thomas thought how beautiful she looked, animated like this. Then she turned to Martin and Annie.

'Martin, what a wonderful suggestion. The Butterfly Farm was perfect. So relaxing, and quiet. But full of life,' she said.

Peggy joined them, carrying Maggie. 'Maggie loved it,' she said. 'A spectacular blue and black butterfly with yellow spots landed on her hand. And she just sat there still as anything ... One actually landed on my nose. There was another one that was the exact color of Emily's hair, a sort of ginger—'

At the same moment, they both noticed the strained look on Thomas's face.

'We should go inside,' Annie said.

'I need to talk to you about what happened to the lights outside your rooms.' Thomas wasn't wasting time.

'It was just a couple of broken bulbs,' Peggy said. 'Kids horsing around. I'm sure you're not happy about it, Martin, but I don't think there's any reason to be too concerned.'

'We don't really have problems like that

here, Peggy,' Martin said. 'But both of your rooms, on the same night – and nowhere else on the grounds.'

'Well, it's kind of isolated down at that end,' Peggy continued, scoffing at Martin's apprehension, 'so it's no surprise...'

Emily realized what Thomas and Martin were getting at. 'You think someone did this to our rooms deliberately.'

'I do,' Thomas said. 'And you have to remember that up until today no one really knew about your connection to—'

'What do you mean, up until today?' Emily asked. 'What's happened?'

'I'm sorry about this, Emily, but Martin's sister-in-law...'

'Oh, no, don't tell me,' Peggy said, her voice echoing the concern in Thomas's voice.

'Peggy, I'd hoped that we could keep some of this information out of the press, at least until we had more to go on, but Joanne told a reporter that you saw the young man with—'

'I never said that, Thomas. I saw *a* young man on the path right before rehearsal and there was something about him, but I didn't see him with Ariana. I...'

'Well, I'm afraid that wasn't Joanne's version. She gave them your name...'

'My name? What's wrong with her?' Peggy instinctively hugged Maggie a little closer to her.

'I'm so sorry, Peggy,' Martin said.

'She only gave them your first name,' Thomas continued, 'but I'd be amazed if they don't have your last name by now ... and she also told them about the bracelet.'

'Oh, no,' Emily said. 'Do they know about where it came from? The inscription?'

'Not yet, but they will shortly. We can't keep that secret anymore. Someone may have seen Ariana wearing the bracelet or know how she got it. We need that information.'

'Then the lights must have been someone looking for information from us, maybe a reporter, someone trying to get pictures. Martin, you said yourself that you were concerned about reporters on the grounds. That's why you got the security...' Peggy said, trailing off.

'No one had this information last night, Peggy. Whoever smashed those lights already knew about you and Emily. And they weren't just looking for information.'

'What do we need to do, Thomas?' Annie said. She knew what was coming, you could tell by her face.

'Martin, Annie, I know you don't want the resort tarnished by the press and I know a police presence will disturb the guests, but I don't think we have much choice at this point. I told the press there would be another update later this afternoon. I'll have to give them the information about the bracelet; they'll already have identified Peggy. They'll have a lot of questions.' He turned to Peggy. 'Just the usual things. Where you're from. Why you're here. How much time did you spend with Ariana? How much time did she spend with the baby? And don't be surprised if there's a picture of Maggie on tomorrow's front page.'

'Oh, Thomas,' Peggy said, discouraged. 'I don't think I can face this. Maybe Ted is right – Maggie and I should head back to New York.'

'Please, Peggy, not until we've had some time to follow up on what you saw.'

'But it was just a young man on the path. He could have been anyone. I assumed he was staff. I thought...'

'But you said something bothered you about him. What was it?'

'Well ... he looked familiar, but that could have been because I had seen him working somewhere. The beach, or the dining room.'

'OK. We'll have you look through the photographs we have of all the staff; maybe you'll recognize him. What else?'

'I know this is going to sound foolish, but when he walked by me he looked away. I mean, he actually averted his eyes. All of the staff here are so friendly, always a greeting and a smile. It just seemed odd. Then when I was walking on, I turned to look back and he was looking back at me. I know it sounds silly, but—'

'There's nothing silly about it. Our instincts are one of the things that often warn us of danger ahead and it's important to listen to them. Now, I'm going to get a sketch artist over here and I'd like you to sit down with him. Let's see if we can come up with something. And I think we need to talk about security,' he said, turning to Martin.

'Absolutely,' Martin said. 'Whatever you think is best. We have a guard at the gate but there are other ways to get on the property.'

'I think we can help out there, but let's leave the same security guard out front. He's good. And we don't want people to become too caught up by the police presence; it will only incite more interest. But...'

'I'm uncomfortable having Peggy, Maggie and Emily remain in those rooms on the bay beach,' Annie said, interrupting Thomas.

'You're right. It's too isolated at that end of the resort ... Maybe the rooms closer to the main house would—'

'No.' Annie was adamant. 'I want them to move up here. I won't take the chance of anything happening to them. I just couldn't...' Tears started to fall from Annie's eyes. She wiped them away quickly. 'I just think it's best,' she said.

'I agree,' Martin said. 'I hope that's all right with you, Peggy?'

'Martin, Annie, thank you, but I just don't think that's necessary. We're fine in our room. Maggie is comfortable there and switching to someplace new ... it would just take so long to get her settled again. If I thought there was something to worry about, believe me, I'd be up here in a flash. But I don't. Anyway, if you're putting on extra security, maybe someone could be assigned to that area. I'm sure that will be enough.'

Martin turned to Emily. 'And you, Emily?'

'I have to agree with Peggy. I can't imagine anyone trying to harm me. I know so little. I'm not so sure about you, Peggy, but are you sure you want to stay down here?'

'I can't see us moving. It's just too much of

a hassle and it will be terrible for Maggie. With extra security, I'm sure it will be fine. And,' she turned pointedly to Thomas, 'it will only be for a short time.'

'Well then, I'll stay down there with you,' Emily said, her voice firm.

'Oh, no! Emily, Maggie,' Annie said. 'I couldn't possibly think of you...'

'Look, Annie, I agree with you, but why don't we talk about this again later? We'll definitely ramp up security down there. Now, I have some calls to make and it would be best if we set up a room to work out of. Martin?'

'Yes, yes, Thomas,' Martin answered, and for just a moment visions of last year passed before his eyes.

'You two must be hungry,' Annie said to Peggy and Emily. 'Why don't I arrange lunch, Thomas?'

'Sorry, Annie. I'd like to talk to Emily for a few minutes and then I have to head back to the Van Meeterens'.'

TWENTY-TWO

Emily and Thomas walked out onto the veranda. They sat at the far end where it was quiet and for a moment Emily just stared out at the ocean. It was clear and sparkling, the sun dancing off each ripple. The waves were high and rolling with a dazzling white spray as they broke. This wasn't an angry sea – its roar was muted. You could imagine riding its swells with abandon.

'You seem discouraged.'

Thomas nodded. 'We just don't seem to have anything solid. Charlie's bar is our best lead, but I'm sure that place was packed on Saturday night. Loads of tourists, and a lot of them young girls. I don't know; it just doesn't seem like Ariana's scene. Something's been going on with her over the last month or so, but ... I wish those friends would talk. Maybe this new girl, Liliana Florek.'

'I keep trying to think of myself at seventeen,' Emily said. 'Who was I? It's hard to remember.'

'And then there's the bracelet,' Thomas said. She wondered if he'd even heard her speak.

Emily thought about the bracelet. She had loved it once. Not anymore. 'I can't believe that Ariana stole that bracelet. It's just not possible. There may have been stuff going on with her recently but I can't imagine that she would do something like that. Why? Why would she do it?'

'I know, it doesn't feel right. That's one of the things I have to talk to Christiaan and Katrien about. Could it be that she has a history of that? We have to know. It won't be an easy conversation but it has to happen.'

'No, you can't avoid that. But I don't think there's anything there. Someone else stole that bracelet, and whoever did gave it to Ariana – and probably killed her.'

'Then it had to be someone who was at the Bluffs,' Thomas said, his face tightening, his eyes intense. 'We've interviewed everyone who was here – guests, staff, day workers, delivery men, everyone. And so far—'

'Nothing,' Emily said.

'There are a few we'll interview again. But no one really stands out.'

'Well, now that you're pretty sure you're looking for a young man – and hopefully Peggy can give some kind of description – you can go back and take a second look at all the young guys you interviewed.'

'We'll do that. Once we have that description. *If* we have the description. But at this point it's all supposition. I just wish we had something solid. If someone stole that bracelet from your room they were pretty clever. There were no fingerprints in there except yours, the woman from housekeeping and the server who dropped off the welcome tray.'

'And I'm sure you've checked them out.'

'Yep. The woman from housekeeping has worked here for twenty years. The server for eleven. Martin swears by them. And they were so upset during the interview. I know they felt threatened – their jobs, their livelihood. Martin reassured them, of course, but still, they were frightened. And there was nothing there. There's no way either of them stole your bracelet.'

'Why do you think the lights were smashed?'

'I won't tell you I'm not worried about that. Someone wanted that area dark last night. Maybe to see better into the suites once the inside lights were on, maybe to scare you and Peggy ... or worse. I don't know. But you and Peggy should reconsider staying in those rooms. I think the two ... the three of you should move up to Annie and Martin's house.'

'I thought about those lights a lot. I just don't think whatever it was, a warning, a threat, was that serious. I don't really know anything, Thomas – I didn't see that young man on the path and I couldn't see who was in the car that picked Ariana up on Friday. I couldn't possibly single him out. Just because I'm identified as the owner of the bracelet doesn't make me a risk to whoever did this. So why would anyone want to break the lights outside my room? No, it must be something else. And Thomas, if Peggy is adamant about staying in her suite, and it sounds like she is, it's much safer if I stay down there with her. Look, Peggy isn't even sure the young man she saw was with Ariana. Hopefully the sketch artist can come up with a decent likeness, but we still don't know if that's him. I think you should clarify that at the news conference.'

'You're right. No sense in people thinking we have an eyewitness when we don't. And that would make me feel better about you staying down by the bay beach. But we can't be sure of any of this, Emily. And I don't want to take any chances. I'll get the security sorted out and someone down there asap.'

'And besides, Thomas, Annie and Martin have enough to deal with right now. Have you looked ... really looked at Annie's face? I don't want to add to that.'

'It's still taking an unnecessary chance, Emily.'

'Let's leave it for now. I promise we'll be careful, and if anything else happens, we'll move.'

'You know once I hold the news conference this afternoon, the press will have your name ... they'll be all over you. And Peggy.'

Emily laughed. 'I know, but I've dealt with that before. And believe me, there's nothing worse than the New York press. I remember one time...' she started, but she could see Thomas had moved on. 'It'll be fine, Thomas.'

'Do you think Ariana had a new boyfriend? I keep thinking about how her friends said she hadn't been hanging around with them as much. Maybe she met someone who was not part of her crowd. Someone local, maybe from San Nicolas, someone a little edgier than her school friends, and that's how she ended up at Charlie's.'

'That certainly would explain it. But some of her friends must know about that. Young girls talk to each other – especially about boys. And you're right; there's a certain lure to the stranger. A little older, more worldly. Probably good looking. For these private school kids who're so sheltered, that can be really tempting.'

'And they don't even know what they're getting into. There's a pretty rough crowd hanging out in some of those bars, especially in San Nicolas. Not so much Charlie's, that's more of a tourist thing, and we're not talking about the hotel bars or the nightclubs. But Black & White, the Java, the American ... there's some pretty rough trade – plenty of booze and drugs. Prostitution. The closer you get to the old refinery, the seedier it gets. It's hard to picture Ariana...'

An image suddenly flashed through Emily's mind: Ariana on the beach. 'Thomas. I just remembered. The afternoon that Ariana came to meet Peggy and Maggie, that first day, on the beach, she went to take Maggie down to the water and started to take off her T-shirt. She had a bruise on her upper arm, like someone had grabbed her. Annie noticed it right away and Ariana made some excuse, something vague ... but she put the T-shirt back on.'

'So if it is a new boyfriend, it's not a very nice one. Time to put some more pressure on those friends.'

Thomas was on his cell phone before he'd even left the veranda. 'Keary,' Emily could hear him say, 'we need to...' And he was gone.

'Has Thomas left?' Annie was standing alone by the door. The others were all seated in the living room.

'He has. He's going to Kat's, then back to headquarters for the five o'clock press conference. I'm not looking forward to that. I'm sure you and Martin feel the same.'

'We'll manage. We'll have to. You know, it's hard to consider anything as too difficult when I see what Christiaan and Kat are going through. Thomas is sending over some support, hopefully in plainclothes, and the forensic guy is going to check out those lights. We'll have the sketch artist come up here. We'll use our office – keep it out of the Reception area. I just wish...'

'We'll be fine down below, Annie.' Emily saw Annie's mouth tighten.

'I wish...'

'Really Annie, Thomas is going to put on increased security – we'll be fine.' Emily hoped she was right.

TWENTY-THREE

He stood at the end of Helfrichstraat, cigarette in his mouth, left hand fiddling with the change in his pocket. He waited impatiently for the contact, late now by twenty minutes. He knew this would be unpleasant, maybe worse than unpleasant, but he was ready – the snub-nose revolver in his right pocket he'd bought six months ago was his insurance. He had asked for the meeting knowing that his plan had fallen through, and knowing he had to put them off. They wouldn't like it, but there was no choice now.

What to tell them? Nothing about Ariana. They didn't know her name, and he couldn't let them think he was connected to her. No, just a change of plans – a postponed trip, two weeks, maybe three. He had this under control. The shipment would go through, just a little later. He'd have to come up with someone else to carry it by then, but it would buy him time. And right now, that was what he desperately needed.

He slouched against an abandoned car and peered across at the old refinery. In its heyday, it had employed most of the workers down here. Now it was an empty shell. This part of San Nicolas was run down and quiet – during the day, at least. Nighttime was a different story. He hadn't really chosen to live down here. It was all he could afford. But he had been so sure that soon he would be making enough to live where he wanted, do what he wanted. He punched the fender. That stupid bitch.

Adolfo wasn't usually late, he thought as his phone rang.

'Yeah,' he said, seeing the caller. 'Where the hell are you?'

He listened for a moment. 'I told Lenny, it's just a delay. Yeah, yeah, I know.' He tried to control his voice but he could hear the slight tremble. 'What the fuck? You told me to set up this deal and it's set. We just have to change the timing ... I know what I said, but the end of the week doesn't work anymore. Hey, what can I tell you, she changed her plans. Tell Lenny there's nothing to worry about...' But Adolfo had hung up.

Billy stomped out his cigarette, ground it into the dirt and headed toward the Java.

The sun beat down on him and swirls of dust kicked up from the road. In a side alley a woman, probably from Colombia or Venezuela, lingered by a back door. She wore satin short-shorts and a halter top, and for a moment she looked hopefully at Billy. There were a lot of these women down here, working. Most operated out of upstairs rooms in the bars, a cut for the owner, stay for a couple of months and then leave. The bar was open, dark inside – there was only one other customer sitting at a table in the back. Time to put his plan into action.

'Hey, Rico, can I get a Balashi,' he said to the bartender cleaning glasses at the sink.

'Billy! Where you been?' Rico said, putting his beer up on the bar.

'You know – around.' Billy took a long swallow of his beer and sighed with satisfaction.

'Lenny was in looking for you last night. Didn't look too happy.'

'Fuck Lenny,' Billy said, slamming the bottle on the bar.

'Hey, hey,' Rico said, holding his hand up. 'Take it easy. I'm just tellin' you.'

'Sorry,' Billy said. He'd come on too strong. 'Lot on my mind.'

'Yeah, know how it is. You workin'?'

'Day stuff, here and there. Waiting to start a new gig. Look, I got a favor to ask. My car's giving me some trouble and I have an interview later over at Eagle. Wondered if I could borrow yours?' he asked. Rico was always good for a favor and Billy had helped him out lots of times. He didn't want to use his own car.

'No problem,' Rico said, putting the keys on the bar. 'I'm here till eleven, so I don't need it. It's in the lot out back. The AC don't work, though.'

'Thanks, Rico. Owe ya one,' Billy said, heading out of the bar.

Step one, he thought, and drove the two blocks to his apartment. Now what?

He'd have to change. Put on his khakis and a shirt. Look like he belonged. Bring a couple of things with him, just in case. Then he'd drive over to the Bluffs.

He'd certainly be stopped at the gate and he was ready. When he got there, it was the same security guard as yesterday. Hopefully he'd remember him.

'Hey there,' he said. 'I'm not sure if you remember me. I was here yesterday for an interview with a Detective Keary?'

The guard nodded but said nothing.

'Problem is, he asked for my driver's license to make a copy and I don't think I got it back. Looked for it everywhere. Must have been left sitting on the desk.'

'OK, just go through to Reception. Someone there can help you.'

'Thanks,' Billy said, driving in through the gates. He parked the car and checked to see if the guard was watching. Luckily, he wasn't. Because Billy wasn't heading into Reception, not just yet.

He walked slowly around the main house. Then he headed to the bay beach. He actually waved to a couple of people in the distance, trying to look like he belonged. They hesitated, but then waved back. So stupid. People always do that – one of those things Billy had picked up early on. They don't want to look like they don't remember you, so they fake it.

He stopped at the beach bar. He would've loved a drink, something to steady his nerves, but he couldn't risk it. They'd ask for a room number and he didn't want to take the chance. Other places, he'd done that. Got a ton of free drinks that way – the bartender would write down the room number and no one would be the wiser until later when the guest complained about the bill.

He sat for a moment, watching the activity on the beach. Not as much fun as watching the girls at Eagle. They were older here and more modestly dressed. Only a few in bikinis, but there was a younger woman a little further down the beach in a neon green one who had a nice rack. He went a little nearer. Sat on the sea wall, figured he'd get a closer look. Hmm, he could watch this one all day, but he had things to do.

'Hi,' he said to the girl behind the desk at Reception. Same one as yesterday. She smiled. 'I was here yesterday for an interview with Detective Keary...'

'Yes, how can I help you?' He couldn't tell if she remembered him or not.

'I ... gave the detective my driver's license and I didn't get it back.'

'Hmm, let me see...' She paused to talk to the porter in the doorway. 'Oh, DJ, those bags go to room 403. Sorry, I thought you knew. Thanks ... Now, where was I?' she said, turning to Billy.

'My driver's license?'

'Oh, right, sorry.' She looked in the cubbyholes on her desk. 'I don't see anything here. Let me check in the office.'

While she checked, he slipped his driver's license in among a pile of papers on her desk.

218

Just in case. Then he watched as the redhead and the one with the baby came down the path that stretched behind the main house. The Maitland's house, he thought. He hadn't even noticed it before but he knew it was up that way. It stood by itself on the bluff.

'Sorry, I don't see it anywhere. If you leave your name and phone number, I'll keep my eye out for it and call you if it turns up.'

'Thanks,' Billy said with a smile. Job done.

He headed outside and watched as she dealt with another guest. Quickly, he got in his car and drove to a back parking lot close to the bay beach – the one used by the staff. There were a decent number of cars here; this one certainly blended in. He jumped into the back seat, stripped off his khakis and shirt and pulled on a bathing suit and T-shirt. If he was going to hang around here for a while he'd better look the part. He needed to get a better look at the bay beach and those rooms down there. How many were there? How close together? He'd only gotten a quick look when he'd broken those lights. It had been dark and he'd had to move fast. And then he'd heard the redhead coming down the path and he'd had to get out of there. He put on a faded Yankees baseball cap and a pair of aviator glasses, picked up the magazine he'd swiped from Reception, slipped the gun into his pocket and casually walked back to the beach.

TWENTY-FOUR

Emily and Peggy ate lunch quickly. They finished just as the sketch artist arrived. Martin showed him into the office and came to get Peggy. The color drained from her face as she left the room. Emily played with Maggie – focusing her attention on the toys scattered on the living-room floor. Annie sat with them, distracted and worried.

'Do you think this will help?' she asked Emily, her voice cracking.

'I hope so. But Thomas thinks they have so little to go on.'

'If there was this new boy, man – whatever – wouldn't Ariana's friends know about it?'

'Some of them must. Thomas said he'll put more pressure on them, but ... If they think that they're protecting her or her reputation, or maybe their own involvement in this, they might not come forward with anything.'

'Well, someone has to make them see! Understand. This is important. This guy is out there and...'

Emily could see the fear in Annie's eyes, looking towards Maggie. 'You're right.' Emily needed to change the subject. 'How are things running down below?'

'They're fine,' Annie said off-handedly. 'Martin and Nelson have everything under control. I suppose I should go down to help, but I just can't seem to get up the energy and—' The phone interrupted. It was strange to see Annie so disinterested in the goings-on at the Bluffs. She stared at the corner of the room as she listened to the voice on the other end. The call finished.

'That was Martin,' she said plainly. 'He has some questions about tonight's dinner menu and there's a mix-up in the rooms.' She paused and then gave a soft smile. 'Things I know he could handle, but I think he feels it's better for me to be doing something. He's probably right. I'll head down to the office. Will you stay until...?'

'I'll wait until Peggy's done. Then I thought I might head to the beach for a while. Maybe Peggy and Maggie will want to go too.'

It was a half hour before Peggy came out of the office with the police artist trailing behind her. He seemed satisfied with the sketch and showed it to Emily – a good-look-ing young man, early twenties, light hair a little too long, wide set eyes and full lips. To Emily, he looked familiar but not really recognizable. She shook her head no.

As soon as he left, Emily turned to Peggy. 'I was going to head down to the beach. Are you going to stay up here at the house?'

'I'm not staying up here! No. No!' She caught herself. 'I'm sorry, didn't mean to sound so sharp. It's just ... I don't want to feel like a prisoner around here. I can see how worried Annie is and, well, I think Mag-gie and I would love to go to the beach.'

They were quiet as they walked down the path. Emily felt unsettled. She couldn't really relax and just enjoy the Bluffs at this point, but there wasn't anything else to do, really. Her mind kept going back to Ariana and the incredible loss that Christiaan and Kat had suffered. It was hard to move on to anything else.

'We're leaving tomorrow,' Peggy said. 'I can't do this anymore. I can't take a chance with Maggie.'

'Does Thomas know?'

'Not yet. I just talked to Ted a little while ago. I haven't told Annie and Martin yet either. That's part of the reason we're not moving up to the house. Just one night ... it's not worth it. It's not that I don't care about what's happened, Emily. But I can't take this kind of risk with Maggie. We're leaving in the afternoon.'

'I understand. Look, let's try to forget all this for a while. Enjoy the sun and the beach.'

Emily headed to her suite to change. Peggy settled herself and Maggie on the sand. The beach was crowded and lively. Things seemed to be getting back to normal. Emily came back and found a lounge chair near Peggy and Maggie. A young man from the beach shack immediately came over with two fluffy blue beach towels. *'Bon tardi,'* he said as he spread one on her chair and left the other rolled at the bottom.

'Danki,' Emily answered.

The sun was bright and there was a soft breeze. Emily looked towards the water. Several brightly striped sunfish sailed lazily along the shore. They reminded her of her morning sailing with Thomas. It was hard to imagine that was just a couple of days ago. She saw Marietta and Nora at the water's edge, doing their usual beach routine – bending down to scoop up a few handfuls of water that they then dribbled on their shoulders and arms. Marietta was wearing her cat's-eye sunglasses and a sheer black sarong over her two-piece bathing suit. Glamorous, as always. Nora wore a practical one-piece, simple and functional. She was a swimmer and a runner, Emily remembered, and her strong, muscled body was proof of that.

As soon as they spotted Emily they walked over.

'Well, my dear! I hope you have lots of sun-screen on,' Marietta said. Turning to Peggy, she added, 'And I certainly hope you're careful with that baby. She shouldn't be in the sun at *all*. The *worst* damage can be done when they're young.'

'Oh, don't worry, Marietta,' Peggy said. 'I'm more than careful. Those swimming clothes, her hat – all UV protection. And she's got SPF fifty all over her.'

Marietta arched an eyebrow. 'It's you, of course,' she whispered, leaning towards Peggy.

Peggy tried to pretend she didn't know what she was talking about, but that would never work with Marietta.

'The witness, that "Peggy". It's you, isn't it?'

Peggy nodded.

'I knew as soon as I heard it on TV. Everyone is talking about it. Of course, Martin's sister-in-law should never have said anything to that reporter. *What* is wrong with her? I can't abide people like that. Always wanting attention, talking about things they know nothing about, and to the press, no less. Don't people realize what happens when they talk to the press?' Emily laughed to hear Marietta speak about the press like this, as she herself wrote a society column in one of New York's newspapers. 'Does she understand *nothing*?'

Maggie poured a shovelful of sand on her head and started to wail. Before Peggy could grab her, Nora had swooped down to pick her up. 'Here, let me take her,' she said to Peggy, and with that she started dusting the sand away and singing a silly song. Maggie immediately started giggling, leaving Peggy at Marietta's mercy.

'Did you recognize the young man?' Marietta asked.

'No, I didn't recognize him. And I didn't see him with Ariana. Joanne got that all wrong. It was just a young man on the path. I didn't see anything. And I think I'd rather not talk about it anymore.'

'Of course, of *course*. How insensitive of me. Bothering you just when you're trying to relax. Well, believe me, I know from experience that Inspector Moller will get to the bottom of this. Isn't that right, Emily? Why, last year—'

'Marietta,' Emily said sternly.

'Oh, there I go again. Well, let's not talk about unpleasant topics. Speaking of Inspector Moller, Emily, tell me, how is that *dalliance* going?'

For a moment, Emily almost wished Marietta would go back to talking about the murder investigation. 'I'm afraid Thomas is too busy to think about any romance right now, Marietta.'

'Pity. I saw the two of you at the wedding. You make a lovely couple. He's so handsome – and so *tall*. Tall enough for you, and that can't be easy to find.'

'*Marietta...*' Nora said, interrupting her singing to Maggie. 'I don't know how you manage it, but you do always tend to put your foot in your mouth.'

'Don't be silly, Nora. Emily knows what I mean. You don't mind my saying that, do you, dear?'

Emily laughed. 'No, Marietta, I don't mind.'

'See, Nora, I told you.'

'Well, I think we've overstayed our welcome,' Nora said, handing Maggie back to Peggy. 'And we wanted to head up to the main house to pick up some more sunscreen before we head back to our room.'

Emily and Peggy laughed as Marietta and Nora walked off. It felt good, Emily thought. They settled down in their lounge chairs, Maggie content to lie quietly in Peggy's lap. Emily checked her watch. 'My God, it's almost four o'clock,' she said.

'That's hard to believe. I'm hoping Maggie will fall asleep here. I might even close my eyes as well. I'm exhausted,' Peggy said, her eyelids already drooping.

Emily watched the crowd contentedly. She could see Martin's sister, Alice, swaying in a nearby hammock, her white beach hat shading her face. Nearby, her husband was stretched out on a lounge chair. His book was overturned on his belly and his eyes were decidedly shut. One of the bar boys came by and picked up the two empty glasses standing in the sand. He walked toward Emily, but she held her finger up to her lips, pointing to Peggy and Maggie. A broad smile covered his face as he made his way to the young man sitting by himself a little further down the beach.

It was strange to see someone alone on the

beach at the Bluffs, a place where couples dominated, but perhaps things were different with the wedding, Emily thought. Like Peggy, not all the guests would have a significant other. She had thought her significant other would be Thomas, but it was clear that, for the second time, Emily would spend most of her stay here alone.

The young man shook his head no to the bar boy. He didn't say anything or smile, just returned to the magazine he was reading. He must be here by himself, Emily thought. No lounge chair next to him; no sense he was waiting for anyone. Occasionally he would pick his head up and look around the beach, but only to observe.

Emily's eyes moved on to a couple closer to the water, their chairs at an angle as if to catch the last of the afternoon sun. The man was dark and muscular, his skin like mocha. The woman was tall and blonde – striking – and it took Emily only a moment to recognize the voluptuous body, slick with oil, concealed only slightly by a neon-green bikini. Emily couldn't help chuckling. Officer Turner. Once again, Thomas had assigned his trusted young officer to keep watch. Clearly, the young man with her was a fellow policeman. Their presence immediately made

Emily feel more comfortable, and no one on the beach would suspect their real purpose.

Billy had picked a lounge chair with the perfect view – to one side the neon-green bikini woman and to the other the redhead and the one with the baby. He couldn't decide which view was better. He pretended to read his magazine but behind his sunglasses his eyes kept a constant vigil. Not much to see, however. They talked to a couple of people – the two old women, the egret and the dumpy one. Dykes, even from here he could tell. Other than that they just sat there. The mother and baby slept for a while. He thought about taking them out here; he could do it. Just shoot and run. The little girl woke up for a moment and played with her mother's hair.

He could see the doors to their rooms, right next to each other. The lights had been fixed. He'd hoped they wouldn't get around to it that quickly; he'd wanted to have some darkness down here after the sun went down, but this was the Bluffs – things like that always got done quickly. It was getting late, the sun was losing some of its heat and guests began gathering up their stuff to head back to their rooms. Soon the beach would be empty and he would have to find a new place to wait.

Peggy and Maggie slept for half an hour, until Peggy woke with a start. 'Oh! Emily, I can't believe I actually fell sound asleep. I had the strangest dream. I was at the airport waiting to get on the plane, only it was all wrong ... it was so dark, full of staircases that went nowhere. And I couldn't find Maggie. I was running up and down calling her name and all of a sudden Ted was there, carrying her, and she was dressed in a Christmas tree costume. Isn't that weird? What time is it?'

'Quarter to five. I was going to head in to watch the press conference.' She paused. 'Do you want to come?' she asked, putting her book in her bag.

Billy was relieved when he saw them gathering their stuff. He had to catch that news conference. As soon as they turned their backs, he started walking casually toward the employee parking lot. He couldn't move his car now – someone might notice. He'd have to walk out. He knew that the press conference was scheduled for five; he needed to hurry. The lot was empty, as usual, so he walked through it, down the dirt roadway and onto the street. He walked to his left, to a broke-down beach bar. He'd been there before and knew they had a TV that hung on the wall. It usually played sports, mostly Caribbean or European soccer, but he knew that everywhere would have the news conference on.

Emily was happy to get into the coolness of the suite. The overhead fan whirled a slight breeze and as always there was a plate with fruit and cheese next to a chilled bottle of white wine on the table. Peggy put Maggie down on the carpet and ran next door to get her formula. While she was gone Emily poured two glasses of wine and turned on the TV.

Thomas's face and voice seemed to fill the room. He looked worn out – eyelids heavy, hair just disheveled enough to give it away. Emily knew he had gotten little sleep. The slowness of the investigation was eating him up. He spoke carefully and deliberately. First, a review of what they knew for sure – which still wasn't that much. Then the possible leads, rumors and suppositions. Here there was more.

Thomas let the reporters know that they were doing extensive interviews with Ariana's friends and classmates. He again called for anyone who had been at Charlie's on Saturday night to contact the police. He tried to dispel some of the more salacious rumors and then moved on to the real meat of the press conference.

First, he released Peggy's full name, though most of the reporters had already figured it out. He corrected Joanne's faulty version of what Peggy had seen, emphasizing several times that she hadn't seen anyone with Ariana. Then he addressed the bracelet. He read out the inscription and revealed the name of the owner. The expected furore ensued. How did the girl get the bracelet? Did someone give it to her? Did she steal it? Did someone else steal it? Had they interviewed people at the Bluffs? Staff? Guests? When did the owner notice it missing?

Emily and Peggy were tense as they watched. They knew this would mean a great deal of unwanted attention at the Bluffs and they could only imagine the stories in tomorrow's papers. Emily dreaded the story of the bracelet being out there, but she dreaded the speculation even more. How could Christiaan and Katrien possibly deal with all of that?

As the reporters shouted their questions,

their voices getting louder and louder as they tried to get Thomas's attention, Peggy realized that Thomas wasn't kidding when he mentioned Maggie's picture being on the front page. These people were ravenous for anything, fact or fiction. It didn't seem to matter.

'I'm glad we're leaving tomorrow,' she said quietly. Emily said nothing.

Thomas ended the press conference with the most important piece of new information – the sketch. The young man, he said, was simply wanted for questioning. He stressed – more than once – that he was not a suspect. It hardly made a difference. The questions poured forth. Any idea who this man was? Was he a friend of the dead girl? Was this the young man seen at the Bluffs? Or had he been seen at Charlie's? Thomas refused to give them much more. He made a plea for the young man, or anyone who recognized him, to please come forward and then left the podium.

TWENTY-FIVE

The minute he saw the sketch, he knew – she had to go. He put the last of his beer down on the bar and looked around. Six people. All of them had just watched that press conference and seen that sketch. Would any of them recognize him? Maybe not now, not yet, but if that sketch was on the front page of the morning papers, soon. Was it a good enough likeness? Probably not with the baseball cap and sunglasses on, but he couldn't wear those forever. And only she could really identify him. The older lady already said she couldn't. The gun itched against his hip.

He left the bar quickly, averting his eyes from the people around him. He headed to the parking lot and quickly changed into his khaki pants and white shirt. That sketch was close, he thought, but probably not close enough. As casually as he could, he walked the narrow path to the service shack behind the main house. Slipping in the side door, he quickly grabbed one of the white polo shirts with the Bluff's staff logo on it. Better. This would probably get him back onto the grounds. For extra insurance, he grabbed a serving tray from a side table on his way back to the car.

Less than two hours till dark. Enough time to get back to his apartment and get what he needed. He had to remind himself to drive slowly. He couldn't get stopped. He could feel his mind speeding up, jumping from one thought to another. His eyes darted around the road before him, searching side roads and oncoming cars. As he reached San Nicolas, he put the baseball cap back on. He scanned the sidewalks and alleys for any sign of the police, and he followed the eyes of every pedestrian. Were people looking at him? Recognizing him?

By the time he got to his apartment, his shirt was soaked with sweat. When Rico said no AC he hadn't thought it would be this bad. But he was smart to be using this car – by the time he got it back to Rico tonight everything would be settled. The sun rippled the sidewalk and its glare stung his eyes as he walked down the deserted street. He knew he only had a short amount of time to pull this off.

It took him just a few minutes to pick up what he needed – dark pants and a black long-sleeved shirt, a length of rope, a knife, a bandana and the truncheon he had picked up in the alley behind Senor Frog's. He threw everything into his backpack and changed into the white Island Bluffs shirt. With the shirt and his khaki pants he'd definitely pass. He dropped a couple of pills in his mouth as he walked out the door and within a few minutes he was whistling as he drove.

Emily and Peggy watched the evening news for a while, anxious to see what kind of reaction the press conference was getting. They showed a clip of Thomas giving Peggy's full name and then, to Peggy and Emily's dismay, a photograph of Peggy and, just as Thomas had predicted, one of Maggie. 'Where the *hell* could they have gotten those photos?' Peggy said, overtaken with alarm. 'I can't believe this.'

The next clip was Thomas talking about the bracelet, followed by a picture of the model and a reading of the inscription. Several people gave their opinion as to how the bracelet might have figured into the story –

whether Ariana might have stolen it, an 'expert' who spoke about kleptomania, and a discussion about whether it could have been given to her. There was a short segment about the Bluffs, with pictures and clips of the previous interview with Joanne Maitland.

The phone rang just as the news ended. 'Emily? It's Annie. We'd like you and Peggy to join us up at the house for dinner. We're serving in the dining room, but we thought you might prefer something quiet.'

'Hold on, Annie. Let me check with Peggy.'

Peggy quickly agreed. 'I couldn't face all those people in the dining room. Everyone staring at us. They don't mean any harm, but it's so uncomfortable.'

Emily let Annie know.

'Good,' Annie said. 'Dinner will be early – six-thirty.'

'We have about a half hour to waste,' Emily said. 'Why don't we take Maggie for a walk before we head up to Annie's?'

The heat of the day had dissipated, accompanied by a pleasant breeze. The sky was turning a deep purple with patches of grey clouds. Emily and Peggy walked the length of the bay beach and then through the garden paths. Without saying anything, they both took care to stay in the lit areas. 'I guess you have no idea where things stand with Thomas?' Peggy asked as they walked.

'No, not at all. I mean, I know things were going well after the wedding. More than well. But since Ariana's body was found there's been ... he's been so busy.'

'But you do care about him?'

'I do. I just wish we could get some time together. I'm sure he does as well. Last night, we walked along the sea wall and just talked. Mostly about the investigation. Then about teenagers, their complications – boyfriends, girlfriends, school. How painful this has been for Kat and Christiaan. How responsible Thomas feels. He would in any case, but here, with the connection to Annie and Martin ... their being such close friends, and now the connection to the Bluffs...'

'I know. It must be so hard for them. Have you noticed any increased security?' For a moment, Peggy sounded frightened. 'I mean, I haven't, but...'

Emily laughed. 'Oh, they're there. If you didn't know you'd never realize ... Did you see the girl on the beach in the neon-green bikini?'

'How could you miss her?' Peggy said. 'I think everyone on the beach noticed her.

239

And the guy with her.'

'Well, those two *are* the extra security. Or at least, part of it.' And then Emily told her the story of how the very voluptuous Miss Turner had actually saved her life last year.

'Wow. Good to know,' Peggy said, smiling. 'I'll make sure I stay real close to her on the beach tomorrow.'

Neither of them noticed the young man who stood watching in the distance by the beach bar. He looked like every other server – a white towel over his arm and two empty glasses balanced on his tray. If they had watched closely though, they would have seen him veer around the bar, place his tray and glasses in a nearby bush and head for the rooms along the beach.

When they reached the house, they found Annie, her brother Christopher and his partner Henri. 'Martin's down in the dining room. I just couldn't face it, not yet,' Annie said. 'I promised him I'd go down tomorrow.'

'I think he's worried about you, Annie,' Christopher said, placing his hand on hers. 'He sees how upset you are … He adores her, you know,' he said, turning to Emily.

'Oh, Chris,' Annie said with a smile, 'stop.'

Dinner was quiet. Maggie was the center of attention as she smeared mashed potatoes on her tray with great concentration.

'Oh, Maggie. No, stop...' Peggy said.

'No, no, leave her,' Henri said with his thick French accent. 'She is painting.'

'Annie, I haven't told you yet, but Maggie and I are leaving tomorrow.'

'Tomorrow?' Annie sounded surprised. 'Have you told Thomas?'

'No. I only made the reservation earlier. Ted wants us home and I don't think I have anything more to offer this investigation.'

'I guess you're right,' Annie said. She didn't sound convinced. 'But...'

'But what if they find someone? I thought about that. I'd come back. I just can't take the chance of anything happening to Maggie. We're not that far – and if Thomas needs me I'll just get on a plane.'

'Of course. You're right. How could you take that kind of chance?' Annie said, looking at Maggie. 'And it isn't that far away, is it?' She paused. 'Will they find someone, do you think?'

'They're certainly trying,' Emily answered honestly. 'They have three-quarters of the force working on this and Thomas has barely slept in the last forty-eight hours. I don't

241

think the rest of them have either. They just need a break. One could come at any time. But it's hard.'

Suddenly Thomas appeared at the front door. 'Thomas,' Annie said, 'we were just talking about you. Come in. Sit down. You look exhausted.'

He really did, Emily thought.

'Let me fix you a plate,' Annie said.

'No, no, Annie,' Thomas said. 'I don't really have time. I just came to check on—'

'Thomas, I won't hear of it,' Annie said, heading towards the kitchen. 'Sit down. You have to eat.'

Thomas came over to Emily and stretched his arms around her. 'How are you?'

'I'm fine. And Annie's right, you have to eat. Please, sit.'

As soon as he sat down, Thomas turned to Peggy. 'Everything OK?'

'Fine. Nothing out of the ordinary.'

'We saw the press conference,' Emily said. 'They certainly are a voracious bunch.'

Thomas gave a sardonic smile. 'They are. I don't mind the questions about the progress we've made. I expect those. It's the rumors. I should be used to it – every time a woman is missing we get the questions about human trafficking. In this case, was it human traf-

242

ficking gone bad. "Gone bad." As if human trafficking can go well.'

'We watched the news after the conference,' Peggy said. 'You were right. There were pictures of both Maggie and me.'

'The French press is just as bad. Maybe worse,' Christopher said.

'I'm sorry, Peggy,' Thomas said. 'Were they old pictures or taken recently?'

'Recently. The one of me was from the wedding and there was one of Maggie in her stroller. They must have figured out my last name and tracked me down.'

Thomas's face fell. 'I don't like that. I'll talk to my people. I thought we had a better perimeter around the Bluffs.'

'I think they might have been taken early this morning. Before the added security.'

'Still, you should rethink staying in—'

'We're leaving, Thomas,' Peggy said quietly. 'Maggie and I.'

For a moment, Thomas looked stunned. From his expression, Emily wondered how much more difficult this was going to make his investigation. His voice sounded disheartened when he spoke. 'Well, I can't say I blame you. And I can't force you to—'

'I'm sorry, Thomas. I just can't take the chance that something might happen to

Maggie.'

'When are you leaving?'

'Late tomorrow afternoon. We have a four o'clock flight.'

'What's happening with the investigation, Thomas?' Emily interrupted. 'Is there anything new?'

'A few things. We have at least four witnesses who saw Ariana at Charlie's after midnight, but no one seems to know who she was with. The place was packed. The bartender said she was doing shots of tequila, but he didn't serve her. Said someone else must have bought them for her. Covering for himself because Ariana clearly looks underage. I'm not sure I believe him. And there's no way for us to know – things are pretty loose in those bars. But if it's true, someone was buying those drinks for her.'

'I just can't imagine Ariana doing shots down at Charlie's bar,' Annie said. 'She's just a child. She *was* ... she was just a child.' Her voice was heavy. 'It seems so unlike her. Were any of her friends with her?'

'It doesn't look like it, not at this point. Hendricks interviewed the Ashruf girl again. Nothing new. And the de Veer girl, also nothing. But that new girl, Liliana Florek, gave us a bit more. Seems she's been covering for Ariana. Saying they were together when they weren't.'

'Does she know who Ariana was with?' Emily asked.

Thomas shook his head. 'She says no. She knew there was a new boyfriend but she didn't know him. Said Ariana was secretive. But she did say that Ariana had been going to Charlie's, and she had mentioned once that she had been to Senor Frogs.' Thomas rubbed his mouth. 'She says that's all she knows.'

He turned to Annie. 'Have you spoken to Kat since the press conference?'

'A little while ago. Their reaction was what you'd expect. All the rumor and speculation is so painful. They don't really put much stock in those stories about human trafficking, although nothing's beyond their imagining at this point. It's this stuff about Charlie's; they just can't imagine her there. But the more they think about this past month – the clues they didn't pick up, the changes in Ariana, the more they believe that there was a new boyfriend. Kat has spoken to some of Ariana's friends, but she hasn't found out much. They all seem to—'

'Believe they're protecting her by not saying anything.' Thomas finished Annie's thought. 'That's always the way.'

'And, of course, there's still the issue of the bracelet. It's haunting them. And that supposed "expert" on kleptomania? Was that really necessary? Children of privilege and all that. Ariana and her sisters were never spoiled. Yes, they had comfortable lives, but they all had part-time jobs, babysat or were counselors in summer camp. Ariana had worked at the orphanage this past summer. She loved it and was wonderful with the kids.'

'There's really no way to stop that stuff,' Thomas said. 'And I'm sure they'll be more of it until we can give them something solid. And who knows when that will be? Well, I'd better head back ... we have a lot to do. Thanks for the food, Annie. And Peggy, maybe we could talk in the morning. We have some new photos to show you – some from Charlie's, some of the day staff and a couple from down by Manchebo. Not much, but worth taking a look at.'

'Of course, Thomas. Whatever I can do. I'm sorry but—'

'I understand and you've been a great help so far.'

'I'll walk you out,' Emily said, getting up from the table.

There wasn't much to say. Emily knew Thomas was disappointed about Peggy leaving. 'She said she'd come back if you needed her.'

'I know she would. It's just that we have so little to go on.' Thomas took Emily in his arms. 'God, I never imagined that our week would end up like this. Will we ever get some time together?' He kissed her and headed out the door.

TWENTY-SIX

'I'm exhausted,' Peggy said as Emily returned. 'I think it's time for Maggie and me to
head back to our room. She's so off her
schedule and I would love for her to get a
good night's sleep ... we have a long day
tomorrow.'

'I'll head back with you. I'm pretty wiped
out myself,' Emily said.

'Well, I think Henri and I will stop down at
the beach bar ... we can walk that far together,' Christopher offered.

Peggy picked Maggie up as Emily started
to clear the table. 'Leave everything,' Annie
said. 'It will give me something to do.'

The sky had clouded over but the night
was still warm. They walked slowly down the
path as Christopher and Henri shared stories of Paris. A *kododo blauw*, a friendly blue-
green lizard, crossed their path and Maggie
let out shrieks of laughter. Suddenly, Emily
was grateful for the company. She was

almost tempted to stop for a drink; it was a relief to be talking about something else and she found that she really enjoyed their company. For a moment, she thought that Peggy, too, might have been tempted. It hadn't been much of a vacation for any of them.

The bar was fairly crowded; it usually was at this time of night, but it was a Monday and Emily was sure it would quieten down soon. Guests sat at tables and talked; a group of young people, friends of Sarah and Jon from New York, stood at the bar. Emily and Peggy waved to people they knew and Marietta came over as soon as she saw them.

'I'm so sorry, my dear,' she said to Peggy. 'This must be awful for you. It's disgraceful, really. Thomas should do something about those reporters,' she continued, turning to Emily. 'And wouldn't I *love* to know how they got those pictures.' She looked over at Joanne Maitland, who sat at a far table with an elderly couple. If looks could kill, Emily thought, as she saw Joanne quickly leave the bar.

'Marietta, come join us for a drink? Emily? Peggy?' Christopher asked.

'Oh, we'd love to,' Marietta answered, waving to Nora to join them.

Peggy hesitated for a moment. 'I'd better

not,' she said. 'Maggie's exhausted and to-morrow—'

'Count me out, too.' Emily tried not to sound disappointed. She would have loved to, but she didn't want Peggy walking back alone.

It grew quieter and quieter as they walked to the end of the bay beach until they were surrounded by only night sounds; even the soft laughter from the bar was gone. The bushes and palm trees cast dark shadows on the edges of the sand and the creaking of a nearby hammock added an eerie note. There were few stars in the sky and the moon was obscured by passing clouds.

'It seems so lonely,' Peggy said. 'I hate to say it, but I can't wait to go home.'

Emily also found herself longing for the lights and bustle of the city.

'Don't get me wrong; I'm glad I came,' Peggy said. 'I couldn't imagine not being at Sarah's wedding, but—'

'I know. It's hard to believe that this has happened. I keep trying to get my mind around it, but ... have you spoken to Sarah?'

'I did earlier. She's devastated, like her mother. Feeling somehow responsible, even though ... but you know, it was their wedding. Christopher told her there were some pictures from the wedding on tonight's news. I can't imagine how—'

'Well, if I read Marietta's look right,' Emily said, 'I think Joanne Maitland is responsible.'

'Ugh. Isn't that incredible? Just what Martin needs. She's despicable. Sarah must have been so upset to see them.'

'How is the restaurant doing?'

'Sarah said they've felt some repercussions – canceled reservations, fewer walk-ins. Not that they care at this point. And if I know people, that won't last long. You know what they say – the only bad publicity is no publicity. Still, it seems so unfair that this should spoil their wedding. Do you think that's all they'll remember when they look back?'

'I hope not. I hope with time they'll be able to recapture the images of their day. It was such a beautiful wedding.'

'It was,' Peggy said as they reached the door to her suite. 'Well, time for us to head to bed. I don't have the energy to do anything tonight. Hopefully, I'll get Maggie to sleep quickly ... maybe read a bit. See you in the morning, Emily.'

'Goodnight, Peggy. Get a good night's sleep. And goodnight to you, little girl,' Emily said as Maggie waved bye-bye and gave her a toothy grin.

Peggy looked around the suite. For a moment she thought of straightening up, picking up the toys on the floor and hanging the shirt that was on the doorknob, but she was just too tired. She turned on the low lamp that stood on the night table, giving the suite a soft glow. Maggie's head rested on her shoulder, her eyes already drooping.

'Come on,' she said. 'Time to get you changed.'

Maggie grinned and giggled as Peggy tickled her belly. She put on Maggie's favorite PJs – white cotton with bright pink bunnies – and then they sat together on the lounge chair as Maggie scoffed down her cookies and milk.

'OK, little girl, bed time,' Peggy said, picking her up and carrying her to the small crib that sat in the alcove. She sang a short lullaby and rubbed Maggie's back, and it was only moments before Maggie fell off to sleep. Peggy tiptoed over to get her own nightgown, trying to not make a sound. She slipped quietly into bed and lay there for a few moments listening to Maggie's gentle, soft snores. Home tomorrow, she thought, and drifted off to sleep, content.

★ ★ ★

Emily put away the clothes she had left out earlier and took a quick shower. The water was warm and drenching, its pressure massaging her weary muscles. She let it pour over her until she felt her body relax and her mind quiet. Getting out, she wrapped a fluffy white towel around her and peered into the mirror. She was taken aback to see the circles under her eyes; circles that mirrored the ones she had noticed tonight on Peggy. She hadn't realized what a toll this was taking on her. She slipped on a short blue nightgown and headed for the chaise longue.

There was a little wine left in the bottle on the nightstand, so she poured herself a glass. She was almost too tired to read so she stretched out, her book in her lap, listening to the night sounds. She loved the bright chirp that she had thought were crickets but Thomas told her were tiny tree frogs. She had looked for them as she walked along the paths, but she had yet to spot one. There must be hundreds of them out there, though, since their song drowned out most others. Once or twice she heard the caw of a large bird and a bit later, she again heard the howling of a dog. It was a mournful sound, a contrast to the bright chirp of the frogs.

She heard the swish of the bushes in the breeze and a branch scratching on glass. At one point she heard a low thump and peered out the window into the black night. As she listened, she almost envied Peggy going home. There was little release from the darkness that surrounded Ariana's murder and she was discouraged about Thomas. It was doubtful they were going to get any time together, and it made her feel small to even be thinking about that in the midst of all this.

Well, no sense dwelling on this; it won't change anything, she thought. I'm exhausted and it's making me maudlin. She would feel differently in the morning. Time to get some sleep. She made her way over to the beautiful four-poster bed, pulled back the white spread and crawled between the soft sheets. She was asleep before her head touched the pillow.

TWENTY-SEVEN

At first, Emily was unsure what woke her up. It was still dark – the middle of the night, but the tree frogs had quit their bright chirping. Her eyes searched the darkness and her ears sought the sound. Crying, she realized, it was just Maggie crying. Poor Peggy, she thought – she had been so hoping that they would both get a good night's sleep. She looked over at the bedside clock: eleven fifteen. She rolled over and closed her eyes, again waiting for Maggie's cries to cease, and after a few minutes she drifted off.

But it wasn't long before she heard the cries again. If anything, they became louder. She got up and looked out the window, but there was nothing out there. After about ten minutes she decided she had to check to make sure nothing was wrong. She threw on her light robe and the sandals that she had left by the door and slipped out into the night. The purple skies had turned black, the

255

moon shrouded by a dark cloud and, except for the baby's cries, everything was silent. She knocked quietly on Peggy's door.

'Peggy, it's Emily. Is everything OK?'

No answer. 'Peggy,' she called a bit louder, but the only response was Maggie's cries as they got shriller. 'Peggy?'

She could wait no longer. She gently turned the knob and stepped into Peggy's suite. She saw Peggy's form lying in the bed. 'Peggy,' she called again, but got no response. She could hear Maggie now, wailing in the alcove. She reached for the switch by the door and turned on the overhead light.

'Oh my God!' she screamed, once, then twice, stunned by the horrific scene before her – Peggy lying among the white sheets, soaked in her own blood. For a moment Emily staggered against the door, turning her face away, unable to move. The blood rushed to her feet, she gagged and felt her head spin. 'No, no, oh my God, no,' she whispered into her hands. Rushing towards the bed, she reached down to touch Peggy's face, only to find it unresponsive.

She ran into the small alcove, picked up the sobbing Maggie and ran out of the suite. 'Help!' she shrieked, her voice shattering the night as she ran down the path. 'Help ... my

God, someone help us.' She stumbled and gripped Maggie to her more tightly. Tears streamed down her face. She ran up to a nearby room and started banging on the door. 'Help, us, please! Someone help us.'

In moments, the area was swarming with people. Guests streamed out of their rooms, most half-dressed. 'What's wrong?' they shouted. 'Who's screaming? What's happened?' Emily crouched on the floor of the nearby room, holding Maggie and trying to calm her. An elderly man, a friend of Annie and Martin's called up to the main house. 'We need help down here!' he yelled. 'The police, an ambulance. We need help!'

But Annie and Martin were already on their way down, racing along the path with the three police officers who had been patrolling the grounds. Annie reached the suite first. 'Emily!' she cried. 'What's...' But she didn't even finish when she saw Maggie in Emily's arms. 'Peggy. My God, Martin, it's Peggy.'

Emily couldn't focus on what was happening around her. She heard the voices and someone asked her a question, but she couldn't understand them. An echo, a scream, reverberated in her head. 'Help us!' it pounded again and again. But whose voice was it? She sat on the floor, her body trembling, her arms encircling Maggie. Someone reached down and tried to take her. 'No, leave her!' Emily cried, rocking back and forth.

'Emily, please.' They reached again.

'I said no.'

Soon Maggie fell asleep and Emily grasped the small white throw that was on the bed. She wrapped it around both of them and for a moment she closed her eyes. She thought it would help her shut out the voices around her, but the image that came to her mind was worse. Peggy covered in blood. Someone had killed Peggy. For a long while she couldn't move. She sat with her head bowed, her hair like a curtain keeping out the world. She stared down at her lap and for the first time noticed the blood on her robe. Peggy's blood.

Someone came and sat next to her. Put an arm around her. 'Emily?' she heard the voice but couldn't recognize it. 'Emily, it's Annie.'

'Annie,' she said reaching out her hand. 'Peggy ... Peggy's covered in blood. Annie, you have to help her.' She reached up her hand, trying to grab Annie's arm.

'I know,' Annie said, pulling Emily close. 'The police are here and the ambulance.

Why don't you let me hold Maggie? That way you can rest a bit.'

Emily nodded her head and released Maggie to Annie's arms. 'What's happened, Annie? What's happened to Peggy?'

Emily got up from the floor and walked to the door of the suite. The scene outside was chaos – police cars and ambulances, their lights flashing, sending streams of color into the night. Uniformed officers carrying flashlights darted in and around the buildings, into the nearby bushes, down to the bay beach. People milled around, voices hushed, eyes haunted. As Emily watched a car pulled up from beyond the beach.

'Everyone, please move back from this area. I know you're all concerned, but please, we have work to do.' Thomas's voice was calm and authoritative. He knew how upset these people were, but he had to get some order here. 'OK,' he yelled, pointing to an officer standing near the door to Emily's suite. 'Move that ambulance over there into the parking lot. Turner is down. Get the medic. Millard, you take over that scene. Once they've moved Turner, comb that parking lot. He must have come in from there, maybe left that way too. Get some lights set up and make sure no one's allowed there but our people.' A uniformed man carrying a large case with EMS on its side moved quickly toward the lot. Two uniformed officers followed him.

'Martin,' Thomas said to a stunned Martin Maitland, who stood with his head bowed just beyond the door to Peggy's suite. 'Martin, I know how this has shaken you, but please, I need your help. We have to get all of these people out of here. We need to search every suite. They all have to be moved somewhere.'

Martin looked startled for a moment, shook his head slightly and turned to Thomas. 'Of course, Thomas, the dining room. I'll send Nelson and some staff up there to get it ready. Best to have them all in one place,' he said, walking off with a determined look on his face.

Thomas turned to his men. 'I want every inch of this resort searched. Keary, take these six men and scour this place, and I mean everywhere. Start with the dining room, now. Then the Maitlands' house. Let me know as soon as the dining room is cleared. Have two men start up there, door to door, every room. Send the guests up to the dining room. No exceptions. No one stays. Hendricks, you get these units here and these people. We need some space to work. Move them out.'

Thomas disappeared into Peggy's suite. Emily could see the shadows of the men inside moving slowly around the bed. She could not help but picture that scene in her head. She saw the flash of a camera, over and over. Soon an older man, carrying a bag, made his way through the door. She recognized him from the news conference – the medical examiner. She turned her face away. Annie sat on the bed with the sleeping Maggie. Tears freely streamed down her face. 'Poor baby,' she said, over and over.

A young police officer stood at the door. He cleared his throat. 'Mrs Maitland,' he said quietly. 'We're moving everyone out of here. Inspector Moller would like you and Miss Harrington to head up to your house. We've cleared it and we have an officer up there.'

For a moment neither Annie nor Emily could say a word. Emily looked at Annie and nodded slightly. Annie turned to the officer. 'Please ask Thomas ... some things ... for the baby.'

He nodded.

The resort was ablaze. There were lights everywhere – every room, every walkway. As soon as Emily and Annie left the suite, they were joined by a very shaken-looking Detective Erasmus. 'I'm sorry,' he said. 'I don't...' He started to say something and then stopped. 'Let's head up to the house. Mrs Maitland, would you like me to take the baby?'

Annie shook her head, no. They walked in silence watching as the police went from room to room and guests headed up to the dining room. Annie was sure that Martin had everything under control. That was his strength. Whenever there had been a problem or crisis over the years, she could always count on Martin to step up. He somehow had that ability to separate himself emotionally from what was going on and find ways to work things out. Of course, there would be no working this out.

When they got to the house they found every light on and a uniformed police officer at the door. Inside, Annie was happy to find her brother, Christopher, and Martin's sister, Alice. Usually she was quite content with the quiet of her own house, but not tonight. Alice motioned to take the baby but Annie shook her head. Maggie had started stirring and Annie wanted to get her to bed. Emily said nothing, still unable to process what had happened.

Annie led Emily into the guest bedroom and nodded towards the bed. Emily slipped off her sandals and, without saying a word, lay down. Annie put Maggie down beside her and placed a rolled-up pillow under the mattress on the other side of the bed. She covered both of them with a light coverlet and turned out the light.

TWENTY-EIGHT

He had to get out of there quickly. The damn baby. He should have gotten her too, but he hesitated when he saw her sitting there in her crib and then it was too late. He couldn't take the chance that someone had heard and was on the way. He ran to the parking lot, turning to see if anyone had spied him. The path was empty but he saw motion at the window of the suite next door. The redhead. He wanted to wait around, but knew it wouldn't be long before she discovered the body.

He passed the cop lying on the ground. That had thrown him. The babe in the neon-green bikini from the beach – a cop? Just shows you can't trust anyone these days. Hope she isn't dead, he thought. Always a mistake to kill a cop. He jumped in the car and turned the key easily. He left the lights off and, trying not to make a sound, drove slowly out of the lot. About two miles down the road he pulled over in a deserted spot right near the water. He quickly stripped out of his black shirt and pants, splattered now with her blood. He rolled them up into a canvas bag and put on his khakis and a blue T-shirt. Checking to see that there were no other cars on the road, he walked over to the edge of the water, put a heavy rock into the bag, tied the top and tossed the thing into the waves below. After that he tossed the knife, throwing it high in the air and watching it arc in the sky then drop quickly in to the water. Little chance of anyone finding that.

He headed back to the Java. He drove fast on the empty road, pushing the car, wanting to get back before Rico went off duty at eleven. He knew he was cutting it close, but even if he was a few minutes late he knew Rico liked to hang out at the bar after work. Free drinks.

When he got to the parking lot, it was almost empty. He pulled the car into a spot, put the keys in the glove compartment and took off. Rico wouldn't even know what time he got back. He walked over to the Bongo Club. It was pretty crowded so no one would recall when he came in, but he made sure the bartender noticed him and a couple of the girls. They'd remember him being there if he needed an alibi. After a couple of minutes he picked up a bleached blonde chica sitting near the bar. He ordered the required drinks, a balashi for him, a white wine for her, and after the second round he handed over the ten bucks to the bartender for the room key and a condom and headed upstairs.

It didn't take long; it usually didn't. These were experienced working girls and time was money. That suited him fine. He'd head back downstairs to the bar and hang out for a while. He'd have a couple of beers and now that he'd already had his chica, they'd leave him alone. Give him some time to think.

The night had gone pretty smoothly. With her out of the way, he thought, he was home free. The car couldn't be traced to him even if someone saw it. And he didn't think anyone did. Anyway, there were thousands of those old beat-up cars on the island. He was careful not to leave any prints behind and he was in and out of that room in two minutes. That sketch wasn't good enough to nail him. And now that was all they had. Except ... that redhead. He was pretty sure there was movement behind those shutters – had she seen him? He couldn't be certain. He'd have to pay careful attention to the news reports.

Any hint of a witness and he'd have to take care of her too.

He was afraid he was going to have to take another trip back to the Bluffs. But at least he didn't have to worry about getting on the grounds. This time, they'd call *him*.

TWENTY-NINE

Emily awoke with a start. The room was dark with just the soft glow of a night light in the corner. For a moment, she couldn't remember where she was, but then it all came crashing back to her. She looked over at the sleeping Maggie and felt tears spilling from her eyes. Quietly, she slipped out of the bed, put her pillow under the mattress and left Maggie nestled among the covers.

She walked slowly to the living room, unsure whether she was ready to see people. But she only found Christopher sitting on a corner of the couch.

She sat down next to him. 'Peggy's dead?' she said, her eyes lowered to the floor.

'She is.' Christopher nodded.

Emily closed her eyes for a moment. 'Do they know who ... what—'

'No,' Christopher said. 'They're still down there ... I don't think they know much. One of the policemen was injured – the one who was guarding the path from the parking lot to the bay beach. She was found unconscious. They took her to the hospital.'

Her? Emily thought. Oh, God, was it Grace Turner? She put her head in her hands and for a moment she could feel the hysteria rising up in her again. She had to get up; she had to move. She quickly walked over to the veranda door and started to open it, but when she saw a figure outside she gasped and slammed it shut.

'It's all right, Emily,' Christopher said, coming over to her. 'It's just a police officer.'

'Are we the only ones here?' She hoped so. Christopher's quiet presence was somehow soothing and it gave her a chance to compose herself. 'How long was I asleep?'

'Just about an hour.'

'What time is it?' Emily had lost all sense of time.

'It's almost three ... Annie and Alice are in the kitchen and Martin is at the main house.'

'What's happening down there?' Emily had seen the lights beyond the veranda.

'I think they've almost finished the search. All the guests are in the dining room. That's where Martin is. He's arranged coffee and drinks and some food. Trying to keep everyone occupied. I don't know how he does it.

I'm sure he can't wait till they can all go back to their rooms.'

'I'm glad it's quiet here. I don't think I could bear noise right now.'

'I'm afraid it won't be quiet for long, Emily. Can I get you something? Coffee, tea, maybe a drink?'

'No, nothing right now, thanks.' She turned and started over to the big easy chair in the corner. She sat and curled her feet under her. 'It's cold in here. Is it cold outside?'

Christopher picked up a throw from the couch and brought it over to her. 'It's a little cool in here – that's the air conditioning. It's still pretty warm outside.' Christopher was sure the cold she was feeling was from shock. 'I think a drink might warm you,' he said. 'A brandy, maybe.'

'We should have moved up here. We never should have stayed down there.'

'Those thoughts won't do any good now.'

'Maybe if I had said I was going to move, Peggy would have too.'

'Emily, don't,' Christopher said, handing her the brandy.

'She said it wasn't worth moving, it would just be for one night. She was going...' Emily dissolved into tears. 'She was going ... home. Said she couldn't stay ... couldn't take that

270

kind of chance with ... with Maggie. We never really thought...'

Annie came into the living room. She looked weary and drawn like the rest of them. 'Emily,' she said, coming over to the chair and reaching her hand out to stroke Emily's hair. 'You're shivering. Let me get you something warmer.'

Annie came back in with a warm robe. 'Here, put this on,' she said, helping Emily into it. She was taken aback by how Emily looked – her skin pale, almost grey, and deep, dark circles under her eyes.

'Oh, Annie, this is my fault,' Emily said, her voice choppy, her thoughts disjointed. 'I should have said ... I could have ... It would have made a difference. Why didn't ... I should have tried to convince Peggy, instead—'

'Emily don't, this is not—'

'We should have listened to you.' She looked up at Annie, her eyes haunted. 'I knew you were worried but we didn't really think ... couldn't imagine that ... Oh, God, why did we stay down there?' Her voice dissolved into sobs.

'Emily, drink some of that,' Christopher said as he got up to pour another brandy, this time for Annie. 'Here, Annie.'

The phone rang and they could hear Alice pick it up in the kitchen. She spoke for a minute or two and then hung up. 'That was Martin,' she said, joining them. 'He said most of the guests were going back to their rooms; the search is finished. The police are going to do some interviews; Nelson set them up in the office. Martin's heading up here and so is Inspector Moller.'

'I suppose Thomas will want to talk to me.' Emily looked wearily at Annie.

'I imagine he will, Emily.'

'I'm just going to check on Maggie.' Emily couldn't face a conversation with Thomas. This was her fault; he had tried to warn her. But she ... they *both* thought the extra security ... Oh, poor Grace.

She headed towards the guest room and quietly opened the door. She could see Maggie curled up sound asleep, her thumb placed securely in her mouth. Emily stepped into the room and closed the door. She walked over and sat on the floor beside the bed. For a few minutes she just sat there, listening to Maggie's steady breathing. She didn't want to talk to Thomas. She didn't want to talk to anyone. She only wanted to stay here in the dark and listen.

It wasn't long before she realized she

couldn't hide here. If they came to look for her they would wake Maggie and she couldn't have that. Somehow she would have to face this. She got up quietly and headed back to the living room just as Martin and Thomas arrived. Martin's face was grey; his eyes bloodshot. Thomas came over to Emily immediately. He put his arms around her and held her close.

'Oh, Thomas, why didn't we listen to you?' Emily said as she started to sob.

Thomas drew her out onto the veranda. 'Give us a minute,' he said to the others.

Emily burrowed into his arms. 'What was wrong with me?' she said. 'I should have—'

'Hush, Emily, don't. I'm the one who should—'

'No, no. I knew you were worried. I should have paid more attention. I just didn't believe anything like this could possibly happen. I thought ... I don't know what I thought. But I should have tried to convince her. And ... and then, when she said she and Maggie were going home, and it would be just for one night, I thought it would be OK ... just one night ... I thought...' She couldn't continue; her body was wracked with sobs.

'Emily, stop. You've got to stop. You aren't to blame for what's happened. Peggy made up her own mind. You didn't make the decision for her. Look, none of us could have known. Yes, I was worried, but even I didn't think ... Hush ... hush,' he said as he held her. 'I've heard from the hospital. We need to go back inside. We need to talk.'

Emily tried to get herself under control. It was clear that Thomas had questions that she had to try to answer. He led her back into the living room. The others sat quietly, no one quite sure what to say. Martin held Annie's hand and put his arm around her shoulder. It was clear she'd been crying again.

'Look, all of you. This has been a terrible tragedy and personally devastating for you, but I need you to answer my questions. As far as we know, you were the last people to see Peggy alive.'

'Can you tell us what happened, Thomas?' Christopher asked.

'At this point, it looks like Peggy was stabbed twice.' Annie and Emily both gasped. It was hard to hear the stark reality. 'She died almost instantly. We'll know more after the autopsy. Now we're trying to piece together a timeline for what happened earlier in the evening.'

'Emily and Peggy left the house right after

dinner,' Annie began, her voice strained.

'OK, I left here about eight, so what time was that?' Thomas asked.

'It was about eight thirty,' Christopher said. 'Henri and I walked with them as far as the beach bar. We stopped to have a drink but Emily and Peggy walked on.'

'We were tempted, but Peggy felt uncomfortable. You know how people are, Thomas – looking and whispering. And she wanted to get Maggie to bed. She wanted them both to get a ... a ... good...' Emily had to stop.

'Did you see anyone on your way, anyone who looked strange, out of place, nervous?'

'Just the usual – guests, wait staff at the bar,' Emily answered.

'Christopher?'

'No one. We had a drink with Marietta and Nora and then headed back to our room.'

'What time was that?'

'That must have been about nine thirty.'

'Were there people still at the bar?'

'Just a few – a young couple who were sitting at the bar talking to the bartender and an older couple who were settling their bill. That was it.'

'Did you go straight to your rooms, Emily? Did you see anyone down that way?'

'We went straight to our rooms and we

didn't see anyone. It's usually quiet down there and tonight it seemed more so. It seemed lonely. As I said, Peggy wanted to get Maggie to bed so they went straight in. I went in, took a quick shower, had a glass of wine and that was it. I didn't hear another sound until...' Her voice cracked.

'OK, Emily, about what time would you say you went to sleep?'

'About nine thirty. It couldn't have been any later than that.'

'I know this is difficult,' Thomas said, his voice softer. 'What was it that woke you up?'

'Maggie,' Emily said, staring straight ahead of her. 'Maggie was crying.'

'No other sounds – footsteps, a door, a car?'

'Nothing. At first, I fell back to sleep; the crying had stopped and I thought ... But then it started again. I got up and looked out through the shutters, but there was nothing. I waited a few minutes and then I started to get worried so I knocked on Peggy's door.' She paused and took a couple of deep breaths. 'When there wasn't any answer, I opened the door and ... that was it.'

'And you're sure you saw and heard nothing other than Maggie crying?'

'Nothing ... Thomas, what happens next? I

276

mean, Maggie...'

For a moment, Thomas's face cracked, then he quickly rubbed his mouth and took a deep breath.

'I've spoken to Peggy's husband,' he said.

'Dear God,' Annie murmured.

'He'll be here around noon. I'll meet him at the airport and bring him here. You can imagine the state he's in. He could barely speak. He said Peggy's sister would come with him.'

'Sarah knows Ted very well and she knows Debbie ... I haven't called Sarah yet. I just couldn't face it, but maybe she could go with you to the airport.'

'Thanks, Annie.'

'As for the investigation, so far there's not much to go on. We're assuming that the guy who did this is the one in the sketch and the one who killed Ariana. So we'll make sure that sketch is everywhere – every store, every bar, every bus station, everywhere. It won't be difficult; this will create an uproar.'

'Does the press know yet?' Martin asked.

'Not yet, but it won't be long. We've gotten a couple of calls asking about a "disturbance" at Island Bluffs. We said "no comment" for now but that won't last much longer. Someone will have seen the ambulances or the medical examiner and, of course, everyone here knows. We'll be lucky if we get till morning.'

'Is everyone finished down below?'

'Not yet, Martin. Forensics is still down there and we're going to close off that area completely. We haven't let those people back in their rooms yet. Nelson is working on relocating them. Also, we're asking that staff not use that parking lot for now. I will tell you it looks like this guy was smart, and lucky – seemed to know where security was set up, walked right into the room, no finger-prints, slipped right back out. We'll look for other traces but, for now, there's not much.'

'Did you arrange to have Maggie's things brought up here?'

'I did. They should be here any minute. Also, your things, Emily. There's no choice now, you have to stay up here. I thought about maybe moving you away from the Bluffs altogether. We do have a safe—'

'No ... I can't do that Thomas. I have to stay here. At least until Maggie—'

'OK, we'll leave that for now. Martin, Annie, I have two officers outside. Also, we are increasing security around the entran-ces.'

Security, Emily thought. 'My God, Thomas, the security ... It was Grace, wasn't it?'

Thomas's face went dark. 'It was, Emily. She was at the service entrance right by the path. He must have come up behind her and—'

'How is she?'

'It's serious, I'm afraid, but Grace is strong. She'll pull through.'

Emily couldn't bear this anymore. 'I'm so terribly sorry.'

'Please Emily, no more. Martin, I hope it won't be too difficult for the guests...'

'I wouldn't worry about that, Thomas. I think a number of them will be leaving tomorrow. Those who can get flights.' Martin looked over at Annie and shrugged his shoulders.

'I'm sorry,' Thomas said. He could only imagine the kind of damage this was causing – the Bluffs meant so much to them.

'It's not your fault, Thomas. And it won't be so bad. Remember, many of the people here are not just guests, but friends and family. I don't worry too much about them. Next week's guests may be a different story. But really, none of that matters right now. Peggy's death seems too much to bear ... for all of us.'

THIRTY

There was very little sleep at Annie and Martin's house that night. Maggie and Emily's things arrived a few minutes after Thomas left, but they just put them in the TV room for now. Emily didn't want to try moving Maggie into the crib for fear of waking her, so they left her in the bed in the guest room and Emily once again lay down beside her. She felt better this way. She knew she wouldn't sleep and she could keep watch over her. After all, Peggy had wanted her to get a good night's sleep.

Annie knew she could no longer put off calling Sarah. She hoped Jon would answer the phone so she could tell him first. Martin sat on the couch beside her as she dialed.

'Jon, it's Annie—'

'Annie, what's wrong?'

'I'm calling with some terrible news, Jon.' Annie could hear Sarah waking in the background. 'Peggy has been murdered.'

'Dear God,' Jon said. 'Hold on, Annie.'

Annie could hear Sarah's voice.

'What's wrong Jon? Who is that?'

'It's your mom, Sarah. I'm afraid she has some...'

Sarah grabbed the phone. 'Mom, Mom, what is it? What's wrong?'

'Sarah, I'm afraid it's ... it's Peggy,' Annie's voice faltered. 'Peggy's—'

'No, don't say it. Please don't. Oh my God—'

'I'm so sorry, honey. I know what good friends you were—'

'What happened? How did this happen?'

'Someone snuck into her suite ... Someone stabbed...'

Sarah dropped the phone and Annie could hear her shrieking in the background. It was several minutes before Jon got back on the line. 'Annie,' he said, 'Sarah wants to come to the house. I think she needs to be—'

'Of course, Jon. We're here. Maggie is up here and Emily too. And Jon, I know Sarah hasn't thought about this yet, but Ted is coming tomorrow, around noon.'

'We should be there shortly. We can talk about it then.'

Annie hung up. 'They're on their way,' she said to Martin.

He sat with his hands held tightly together. Then unclasping them, he rubbed his eyes and then his cheeks. 'Maybe we should close the resort, Annie?'

'Martin, what are you saying?'

'I don't know. I'm just thinking ... maybe we need to take some time ... to think about this whole—'

'Martin, you love the Bluffs. You've spent your whole life creating a place where—'

'I know, I know but maybe it's time to—'

'No, we're not making a decision like that at a time like this. Look, you said many of the guests were leaving. I don't blame them. And frankly it will be better for us. I don't know how you've been dealing with this. I know I can't—'

'This has been a lot harder for you Annie ... with Kat and all.'

'Once everyone leaves, it will give us some time to ... think ... to plan for—'

'I can't, Annie.'

Annie was taken aback at how panicked she was hearing Martin. The Bluffs had been their whole lives. What would they do? Where would they go?

'No, Martin. This isn't the time for making that decision. But you're right. We need some time and space. Tomorrow, after the guests have checked out, we'll begin calling those who have reservations for the next couple of weeks and tell them we're closing temporarily. I'm sure they'll understand. I'm sure many of them will be happy; it will save them from having to call us and cancel their reservations. Once people hear—'

'We could try to set them up in other resorts,' Martin said. 'I know it's a busy time in January, but you know everyone holds back some last-minute rooms in case ... I'm sure, under the circumstances, they would help out.'

'All right,' Annie said, anxious to get started. Suddenly the thought of some time away from the Bluffs consumed her. 'So in the morning, we'll have Penny draw up...' But her words were interrupted by Sarah and Jon's arrival.

Emily awoke to a gentle tugging on her hair and opened her eyes to find Maggie lying next to her. Once again the reality of what had happened last night flooded back to her and for a moment she could feel the sob in her throat. But she didn't have the luxury of breaking down this morning; she had Maggie to think about.

'Good morning, sweetheart,' she said very

gently, smiling and reaching over to stroke the side of the baby's face. Maggie giggled and Emily softly tickled her belly. They lay there playing for a few minutes as Maggie gurgled and babbled and then Emily picked her up and said, 'Want to get up, little girl?'

She carried her over to the window and they both looked out at a bird that was perched in a nearby tree. Emily noticed some diapers and an outfit for Maggie on the nearby bureau. Annie must have put them there; she must have come in during the night. Emily was amazed that she had slept at all, let alone slept that soundly.

She carried Maggie over to the bureau and got her changed, all the while singing silly songs. Then she put on her robe and headed out to the living room.

As soon as Sarah saw them, she started to cry. 'Sarah, you can't,' Annie said. 'We talked about this.'

Sarah turned away to wipe her tears. 'I know,' she said, getting up from the couch. 'Hey, Maggie,' she said, reaching out to her with a smile. Maggie seemed delighted to see her and so was Emily. Maggie needed a familiar face right now and Sarah offered her that. 'Come on, little girl, you must be hungry.' Annie and Emily stayed in the living room as they went into the kitchen. They all sensed that too many people might over-whelm Maggie. Best to keep things as easy and comfortable as they could.

The morning went by quickly. Annie went down to the office to help with the guests. They needed to see who they could get plane reservations for and who needed cars to the airport. Thomas had cleared them all. He knew his killer was not here. Annie hoped that many of them would be leaving. The thought of the Bluffs being empty was strangely comforting. Emily and Sarah spent their time playing with Maggie. Occasion-ally, Maggie would look around, her eyes questioning and a slight quiver on her lips. 'Mama,' she would say. 'Mama?' Emily and Sarah would distract her with a toy or a game and, for that moment, she would for-get.

Neither of them wanted to watch the morning's press conference. Thomas entered the room and headed straight for the podium. There was barely room for the re-porters to stand, it was so crowded. Thomas could see the usual local press people massed in front; they must have gotten here early. To the sides and in back were repre-sentatives of the international press. Thomas recognized the stringers from the *New York Times* and the *New York Post*. He already knew he would hate seeing that headline. Photographers packed the room, their cameras clicking incessantly. Between the bodies and the lights, it was stifling.

He tried to make his statement as brief as possible. The facts about what had occurred at the Bluffs, their assumption that the killer was also the killer of Ariana Van Meeterens, the little information they had and how the investigation would proceed. He stressed the importance of the sketch and held it up, giving everyone a chance to see it. Fliers would be widely distributed. Anyone who thought they recognized the suspect, please contact the police.

The moment he finished, the room erupted. How had she died? Thomas reported what they knew, but said the medical examiner would have further results after the autopsy. Time of death? Sometime between nine thirty and eleven thirty last night. What about the baby? Safe. The father was coming from New York later in the day. Thomas implied late afternoon; he desperately wanted to avoid a scrum of press at the airport. Any witnesses? They were following a number of leads, Thomas said vaguely. Condition of the policewoman? Critical. The questions were endless. Anything new in the Van Meeterens' murder? Also following leads. Was she at Charlie's that night? It seemed so. They were talking to witnesses. What about the brace-let? Nothing new. Thomas let it go on for as long as he could and then ended it as he had the others – reminding everyone about the sketch and promising another press confer-ence later in the day.

As soon as the klieg lights went out, they all scattered, some to file stories and some to try to track down leads. When he looked out the window of his office, he saw reporters doing their stand-up commentary – CNN, ABC, CBS, NBC and any number of others. This story would travel around the world in a matter of minutes.

It didn't have far to travel to reach Billy Dunlop. He sat in his tiny apartment on Helfrichstraat, his eyes riveted on the TV. He listened carefully to what was said, trying to read between the lines. It sounded like they didn't have much, except for the sketch. He stared at it as Moller held it up, then walked over to the mirror and stared at his face. He was right – close, but not close enough. He didn't like the answer to the question about witnesses. The guy was being evasive. Could he have been seen? Did they have a witness? The only one could be that redhead. And why couldn't they just let go of the bracelet? Billy knew that was trouble for him.

He lit a cigarette and tried to figure out what to do. He knew he was risking everything, but he couldn't take the chance that she had seen him ... And what if she remembered about the bracelet? No, he had to get rid of her. He quickly came up with a plan, rough but possible, and it involved getting back into the Bluffs. He knew the place would be crawling with cops, but he had thought ahead and his first step was already in motion.

Around eleven, Sarah got ready to go to the airport with Thomas, a trip she was dreading. 'I don't know how I'll face him,' she said to Emily, but there was little time or space to dwell on it. Emily decided to take Maggie for a walk in the stroller; she didn't want her to see Sarah leave. One of the police officers attempted to follow them but Emily waved him away. 'We're just going down to the main house,' she called. 'We'll be fine.' She could see him talk into his walkie-talkie as they started out.

They headed down the path and Emily could see the guests streaming in and out. She knew Annie and Martin were trying to arrange flights for those who were leaving and from what Annie had said, that was most of the remaining guests. It would be strange to see the Bluffs empty. She would stay the few days until her scheduled flight on Friday.

Emily walked down towards the beach bar. There were a few people sitting at the tables having an early lunch. Almost all of them were wearing long pants and sensible shoes – a sure sign in the Caribbean that you were heading home. She heard footsteps behind her and turned to see Marietta and Nora. 'Oh, my dear, I'm so sorry,' Marietta said. For once she was quiet, almost at a loss for words. She looked down at Maggie, smiled for a moment and Maggie smiled back, but Marietta had to turn away with tears in her eyes.

'Are you heading home?' Emily asked.

'Not today,' Nora said. 'It's just too complicated making new arrangements. We were leaving tomorrow anyway ... and we thought Annie and Martin could use some support. This is so difficult for them.'

'It looks like most people are leaving,'

Marietta said, regaining her composure. 'A few are switching to different resorts, mostly those who were staying through the weekend. Everyone is being very good about it – after all, these are old friends.' She stopped and looked around her. 'You know, I've been all over the world – great cities like London, Paris and Rome and small towns, rural and remote. I've been to the mountains in Switzerland and the islands in the South Pacific but this, the Bluffs, has always been home. The place I come to be myself, to rest and rejuvenate. I *hope* it will still be here when this is all over.' She turned to Emily. 'Will you go?'

Emily shook her head. 'No. I'll stay till Friday.'

Maggie started making noises in the stroller. 'I'd better keep moving,' Emily said. Marietta leaned towards her and hugged her. 'It's all *too* terribly sad, isn't it?' she said, as she and Nora headed for a nearby table.

Emily looked beyond the beach bar and saw the deserted bay beach. Strange to see all the vacant lounge chairs. No one snorkeled offshore, the small sail boats and kayaks were all pulled up on the sand and the empty hammocks swayed slowly in the breeze. At the end of the beach Emily could see the yellow tape that cordoned off the rooms. A young police officer stood guard on the path. Yes, it was all too terribly sad, Emily thought, and headed back towards the house.

It was empty when she got back there. Empty and quiet. She made Maggie a peanut butter and jelly sandwich and went out on the veranda. She spread a blanket on the floor, grabbed a couple of toys and a bright orange ball and played with her there. She knew it wouldn't be long before Ted arrived.

Emily saw them a few minutes later. They didn't come to the house first but headed down to the bay beach. Ted and Thomas walked ahead and Sarah and another young woman followed. Their bent heads and hesitant walk bore out the anguish of this journey. They spent just a short time down there then turned and headed to the house.

Emily met them at the door, holding Maggie in her arms. Their faces were a map of grief, every line and crevice etched with unbearable sorrow. Maggie reached out to Ted. 'Dada,' she cried as he held his arms out to her. For a moment, as he held her, he sobbed. Maggie looked like she was about to cry too, but Ted stopped himself and, wiping away his tears, he lifted her high in the air. 'Cupcake,' he said, and Maggie laughed.

Emily headed into the den knowing that it was best to give Ted and Peggy's sister time with Maggie. Sarah went into the kitchen to make lunch, even though everyone said they weren't hungry. 'I'll just do light sandwiches,' she said, sounding just like her mother. Thomas followed Emily into the den.

'How are you?' he asked.

'I'm sure I'm doing better than you at this point. That must have been a terrible journey.'

'It was, but I think Ted is strong and he has Maggie to take care of. He's committed to doing whatever needs to be done to help her get through this. It's so hard; you can't even explain it to her. There really are no words for a baby so young ... Has everything been quiet here?'

'It has. Too quiet. Oh, there's been no sign of anything suspicious if that's what you're asking, but I'm afraid the Bluffs is starting to feel desolate. Annie and Martin are at the main house; they asked that you let them know when you arrive.'

'I will. Let's give Ted and Maggie a little longer ... You're being careful, Emily? Please don't take any chances. No walks off the grounds and really you shouldn't go out alone, particularly now that the place is starting to empty out.'

'How did the press conference go?'

'Like you'd imagine. This is international news now.'

'The pressure on you must be awful.'

Thomas just shrugged but Emily could tell from the lines on his face that the stress was almost overwhelming. He took out his phone and called down to Reception. 'Annie, we're here,' Emily heard him say. 'Ted is with Maggie and Peggy's sister Debbie. Sarah is making some lunch ... OK, see you in a few minutes.'

Annie called to Martin who was in the office. 'They're here, Martin ... they're up at the house.'

Martin sighed and for a moment held his head in his hands. 'Best we go up then,' he said.

'I'm fine here, Annie,' Penny said. 'It's lunchtime and almost everyone is heading to the restaurant. Things should be quiet for a while.' She straightened the pile of papers on her desk and out fell what looked like a small card. 'Oh, damn, how did that get in there?'

'What is it?' Annie asked.

'It's just a driver's license. One of the day staff left it behind ... No problem. I have his number. I'll just give him a call.'

THIRTY-ONE

Thomas returned to headquarters and Emily walked him as far as Reception. He put his arms around her before he left. 'Emily, there's something...' he began and then stopped. 'Promise me you'll be careful.'

'I will, Thomas, and I'm sure your men are keeping a good eye out.' She kissed him gently on the lips as he turned to go.

Lunch was a somber affair, except for Maggie, who was clearly happy to have her father here. A couple of times she looked around questioningly and said 'Mama' but Ted just replied 'later' and distracted her. Everyone tried their best, but there was little to talk about and even less emotional energy to do any talking. They ate little and were soon ready to leave. Annie had packed Maggie's things in a small suitcase and gathered most of her toys into a bag. Sarah was driving them to a secluded, small beach house a couple of miles from the Bluffs where they would stay for a few days.

Annie and Martin headed back down to Reception. 'Did you get that young man?' Annie asked Penny.

'I did. He'll come by to pick it up later this afternoon. I should still be here, but just in case I'll put it in this first cubbyhole here, and I'll let the officer at the gate know.'

Emily was not sure what to do. Now that Maggie was gone, there seemed no reason to try to keep a game face on. For a while she just sat in the living room, looking out at the veranda. Every few minutes she would see the police officer who was stationed outside the house making his rounds. She tried watching television but there seemed to be nothing other than news of Peggy's murder. After a while she decided to move her clothes out of the TV room and into the guest room.

She looked at the lovely dresses she had brought for what she had believed would be romantic dinners. She didn't bother to hang them up, just folded them and put them in her suitcase. She put her bathing suits in the drawer, although it was doubtful she would go to the beach again, and certainly not the bay beach at the Bluffs. It was when she went to hang up her navy blue blazer that she remembered – the blazer, the airport ... the bangle. The young man at the airport, it had to be. Her bangles had been in her blazer pocket; she hadn't packed them with her other jewelry.

Oh, God, she had to get to Thomas. She called headquarters in Oranjestad.

'May I speak to Inspector Moller, please?'

'Who's calling?'

'Emily Harrington.'

'Ms Harrington, can you tell me what...' Thomas overheard Hendricks talking into the phone and grabbed it.

'Emily, what's wrong?' he said, fearing the worst.

'Nothing, nothing's wrong ... Thomas, I just remembered ... I remembered about the bracelet.'

She quickly told Thomas the story about the bangles being in her pocket and the young man who had bumped into her at the airport. No sooner had she finished than Thomas said, 'I'm on my way. I'll be there in fifteen minutes. Meet me at Reception.'

Emily quickly changed and headed down to Reception. Annie sat at the desk with Penny standing behind her. Martin was in the office trying to make arrangements for the couple who sat in the nearby chairs. 'My

God, Annie, I remembered,' Emily called out as she entered the room. 'I remembered about the bracelet.'

Martin dropped the phone and came running out just as Thomas arrived.

'What are you saying?' he said. 'What about the bracelet?'

'No time to explain now,' Thomas said, grabbing Emily's hand. 'We have to head to the airport. We may have him.' And with that they ran out the door.

The ride to the airport was swift. Thomas stuck a flashing light on the car's roof and used his horn liberally to get through the late afternoon traffic. Emily recounted the story of the bracelets once again.

'I totally forgot about the incident. It happened so fast. I didn't even remember that the bangles were in my blazer pocket. I had stuck them in there when I was leaving my apartment. When that guy bumped into me the blazer fell to the ground. He picked it up and that's when...'

'Did you get a good look at him?'

'No, I was bending down to pick up my bag ... but Peggy ... Peggy yelled at him.'

'Did he look at all like the guy in the sketch?'

'I'm not sure ... maybe.'

They pulled up outside airport security and raced inside. Thomas flashed his badge as they entered the room.

'Chief Inspector Thomas Moller,' he said. 'I need to see all the CCTV tapes from Friday. What time, Emily? What time did your flight arrive?'

'Around twelve thirty,' Emily answered. 'The airport was crowded; lots of flights arriving.'

The first two tapes yielded nothing, no sign of Emily, Peggy or the young man. But the third one had it – a clear picture of the good-looking young man with the slightly shaggy blond hair, knocking into Emily and her jacket falling to the floor. 'There,' Emily said. 'There he is. Just then, that must have been when he stole the bangles. Oh, God, that's him.'

Thomas looked carefully at the tape. 'Close enough to the sketch. That's him, all right.'

'We need to take this,' Thomas said to the security officer. 'And save all the rest of them from that time period. I'll send someone to pick them up.'

They headed back to the station and Thomas displayed the tape on a monitor in his office. Millard and Keary viewed it with him.

'I know that guy,' Keary said as soon as the picture flashed on the screen. 'He was one of the day staff that I interviewed. Wait.'

He went to his desk and pulled out the book with the information. 'Here he is,' he said showing them the copy of the license.

'That's him,' Thomas said. 'OK, Emily, I'm going to get someone to drive you back to the Bluffs. You can't be part of this. I'll let you know when we've picked him up.'

It was strange to feel the sense of elation that Emily felt. It was somehow like she had won; she had beaten him. It didn't change the tragedy that had occurred, but Emily couldn't help but feel a certain triumph.

She went to Reception as soon as she reached the Bluffs. Annie and Martin were anxiously waiting for news.

'Emily,' they both said as she walked in. 'What's happened?'

'I remembered. The bracelet. I hadn't packed it with my other jewelry. I'd put it in my blazer pocket and then, at the airport, this young man ... him ... it was him. He bumped into me, knocking my bag and blazer to the ground. He picked it up and threw it back to me. That must have been when he stole the bracelets.'

'Oh, thank God,' Annie said. 'Do they

know who he is?'

'They think so. Thomas said they were going to pick him up. Oh, Annie, I know it doesn't really change what's happened but I just feel—'

'I understand, believe me,' Annie said, hugging her.

'Thomas said he would call when they got him.' Emily suddenly felt exhausted. So much had happened in the last twenty-four hours. Suddenly she didn't think she had the strength to even stand. The room began to spin slightly and she grabbed hold of the desk.

'Emily, are you all right?' Annie asked.

'I just suddenly feel ... I think I need to lie down.'

'I'll walk you up to the house. Of course this has all been overwhelming for you. You need to rest ... Martin, I'll be back down shortly.'

Everything seemed strangely quiet as they walked up the path. 'Has everyone gone?' Emily asked.

'Not quite everyone, but a good number. Some have headed home and a few to near-by resorts. Everyone has been lovely about it – except Joanne, of course.' Annie shook her head. 'You would think all of this happened just to inconvenience her ... There are a couple of people still here – Marietta and Nora, and Christopher and Henri, Alice and Joe and a few others. They'll be a small group in the dining room tonight. We'll serve an early dinner. I'm sure everyone needs their rest ... which is just what you need.'

'I wanted to wait for Thomas's call. I'm sure—'

'I'm sure it will be a while before that call comes, Emily. You lie down. If Thomas calls, I'll wake you. You can hardly stand up.'

'You're right, Annie. Promise you'll wake me?' she said as she opened the door.

THIRTY-TWO

Thomas flew into action. 'OK, we have his address so let's go. I want four unmarked cars, no sirens, no lights. I don't want this guy to see us coming. Keary, I want you in jeans and a T-shirt. You'll go in first. Take Bermudez with you. Someone pull up the map of San Nicolas. Zoom in on Helfrich-straat.'

'I got it,' Millard said.

'OK, not much there. End of the street. That's it, number thirty-six. Small building, near the refinery. Looks like a store on the first floor. Someone find out what kind of store that is. He must be on the second floor. Hendricks, get me a couple of marksmen and a negotiator. This guy won't come easy.'

Billy got the call about three o'clock. He answered his phone on the second ring. 'Hello.'

'Is this William Dunlop?' It was the girl

from Reception at the Bluffs.

'It is.'

'Hi, Mr Dunlop. This is Penny, the receptionist at the Bluffs.'

'Oh, hi.'

'I've found your license. Sorry, I should have noticed it yesterday. It was mixed up among a pile of papers on my desk.'

'That's great. I was beginning to give up on that. Thanks so much. Look, I'm at work right now. Can I pick it up later this afternoon, say about four-thirty or five?'

'No problem. I'll let them know at the gate that you're coming.'

Billy smiled; his plan had worked.

Thomas organized his men. Four cars, two in each. 'And I want back up ready. Three police cars. Let's use the bus stations. One at Bernard, one at Nicolas and one at Lago.'

'You want me and Bermudez in first, right?' Keary said, the two of them appearing in scruffy jeans and T-shirts.

'Yeah. There's a small bodega on the bottom floor. You and Bermudez go in, check it out. If it's empty, talk to the owner. Find out what you can about Dunlop. See if this guy knows if he's there. Either way, get the owner out of there. As soon as we see him come out, Hendricks and I will head in. I want one of those marksmen across the street, in this building here.' Thomas pointed to a derelict building directly across for Dunlop's. 'And one in the alley around back. Make sure he's not seen.'

It took about twenty minutes to get to San Nicolas. The streets were almost totally empty and dusk was coming fast. Two local prostitutes hung out in a nearby alley. Thomas hustled them along. As soon as everyone was in place, Keary and Bermudez entered the store. Thomas and Hendricks waited in a doorway down the street. It took only a few minutes for the owner to come out. Thomas signaled to Millard to pick him up and he and Hendricks headed in.

Billy dressed in his khakis and a white shirt. He put what he needed in a backpack that he slung casually over his shoulder. He had to travel light today. He borrowed Rico's car again and drove slowly to the Bluffs. The sun's heat scorched the car and sweat trickled down his neck. He wasn't in any rush. He was waiting for the day's light to start to fade. As soon as he pulled up to the gates, the policeman held up his hand and walked over to the driver's window. Billy was ready.

'Hi, Officer. My name is William Dunlop. I'm here to pick up my driver's license.'

'Right. Penny called down earlier. OK, you can head in. It's at Reception but you'll have to park in the far lot; the other one is closed.'

'No problem. Thanks.'

'OK,' Keary said as Thomas entered the bodega. 'Dunlop lives alone. Few visitors. Often home during the day, sometimes works nights. The guy isn't sure if Dunlop's home. Hasn't seen him since yesterday. Not unusual, doesn't see a lot of him. This is the only way in or out. Stairway is over there. The apartment is small – one room and a bathroom.'

Thomas and Keary quietly made their way up the stairs. Thomas could feel his pulse quicken. The sweat trickled down onto his collar. Damn, it was hot in here, he thought. When they reached Dunlop's door they positioned themselves on either side. Then, with guns drawn, Thomas kicked it in.

Empty. No sign of Dunlop. The room was spare – a ratty old couch, a bed against one wall and a small kitchen unit at the other end. They quickly made their way over to the bathroom and kicked in that door too. No one. Dunlop wasn't here.

Billy parked the car and grabbed his back-pack. Parking here worked out great. Gave him a chance to walk around a bit. The place was like a ghost town. Nobody out. Beach bar empty. He could see the yellow police tape that cordoned off the bay beach and all the rooms down there. He headed to the main house.

'Hey,' he said with a friendly smile as he walked in. She was by herself at the desk.

'Oh, hi,' Penny said. 'Sorry you had to come all the way back here...' She was inter-rupted by the Maitland woman.

'Penny, Emily's lying down up at the house. I'm going to help Martin finish up. Please let me know if Thomas calls.'

'Sure, Annie.'

She turned back to him with an apologetic smile. 'Don't know how I missed this. Things are a little crazy here.' She handed Billy the license.

'I can imagine. Well, thanks for finding this. I thought I was going to have to go through the hassle of getting a new one. What a pain.' He was too nervous to make any more small talk. He couldn't believe how his luck was holding out. So, she was up in their house. Good ... a quiet spot, sort of hidden. He left the office with a smile and a wave.

'Damn,' Thomas yelled, maddened and exasperated. 'OK, Hendricks, you take the room, see what you can find. I want to know whatever there is to know about this guy. Any links to the Van Meeterens girl or Peggy Lawson, bag it. I'll send one of the uniforms up here to help you and post one down-stairs.' Hendricks immediately started to tape up the room. 'Don't put any tape out-side in case he comes back. Don't want to scare him off. I'll put a couple of plain-clothes guys in the area.'

'Right, Chief,' Hendricks said.

'Keary, you and Bermudez start canvassing the neighborhood. I want everything. Find out where he hangs out, who his friends are, what he's involved in. And start cracking some heads. I'm sure this guy is into the drug trade, or wants to be. Put some pres-sure on the regulars, see what turns up. I'm heading over to the Bluffs. If this guy is on the move, we need to find him and fast.'

Billy headed straight for the beach bar. Even though it was empty, the men's room was open. He ducked in there and changed into jeans and a dark long-sleeved shirt. He put the gun in his pocket and stuffed his clothes in the backpack. All set, he thought, but it was too soon to head out. He waited patiently for the sky to darken.

Thomas pulled up to the entrance of the Bluffs and flashed his badge at the police-man at the gates. 'OK, no one in or out of here until I say so,' he said, driving through.

It was dark now. The resort was almost empty. There were no guests walking on the pathways or sitting at the beach bar. It was so strange to see it so quiet. He could see the lights on in Reception. Annie, Martin and Penny sat working at the desk sifting through a pile of registration slips.

'Thomas!' Annie cried as he entered. 'What's happening? Emily said you—'

'We know who he is,' Thomas said, pulling out the picture of Dunlop and putting it down on the desk. 'William Thomas Dunlop ... he was day staff here on Friday. I'm clos-ing off the grounds, no one in or out until we find this guy. I want—'

Penny's face drained of color. 'Oh my God, it's him. Oh, God, I'm sorry ... it's him ... he's here. He's here already.'

'What are you talking about? How—'

'He left his driver's license behind. He said he ... he came to pick it up. I'm sorry. I didn't know...'

'How long ago?'

'Forty-five minutes, an hour? I can't be sure. He—'

'Where's Emily?' Thomas said, turning to Annie.

'She's up at the house.'

'OK, Martin. I need you to call Detective Keary. Tell him Dunlop is here, somewhere on the grounds. Tell him to contact everyone we have stationed here and let them know. And tell him to get that team over here.'

Billy stood silently in the bushes outside the house. The lights were on inside and he had an unspoiled view. He was dying for a cigarette, just a couple of drags. For a moment, he fingered the lighter in his pocket, but he didn't dare. He moved slowly around the house, searching for her. The rooms at the back were dark, bedrooms probably. Then a light came on. He crept closer. He knew she couldn't see him. It was too dark out here.

He watched as she stripped off the rumpled slacks and blouse she had been wearing and put on a pair of shorts and a shirt. Damn she was hot, he thought. Too bad. His

eyes followed her as she left the bedroom.
For a few minutes, she walked around the
house. She headed into the kitchen; poured
a glass of water, took a sip, then poured the
rest out. He watched as she looked at some
photographs on an end table in the living
room. She picked one up to look at it more
closely and then put it back down. She
looked unsettled, moving from the dining
room to the TV room. He edged along following her every move. A young cop knocked on the veranda door. He ducked down.
She started, peered out and slid open the
door.

'Everything OK, Miss Harrington?' he asked.

'Oh, I'm sorry. Fine ... fine. Thank you,
everything's fine,' she said, but Billy could
see she was nervous. The young cop walked
away, making his rounds to the back of the
house, but she didn't close the door. She just
stood there looking out into the night. This
might be my only chance, he thought as he
raised his gun.

Thomas raced up the path to Annie and
Martin's house. The outside was shrouded in
darkness, but he could see the inside lights
blazing in the night. And there, standing in

310

the living room, was Emily – a perfect target.

He crept silently along, searching the near-by bushes and shrubs. There was little sound, even the night creatures were silent. And then ahead of him he heard a rustle. There, in the bushes to the left. A figure was rising up. A hand reaching out, holding a gun.

'Emily, get down!' he roared.

He heard a shot. Saw Emily diving to the floor. The figure turning. Another shot, then another. And then it was done.

THIRTY-THREE

Emily threw herself to the floor when she heard Thomas's roar. She could feel the bullet whizzing past her as she lay there frozen, her heart pounding and her breath ragged. She rolled to the shelter of the sofa, holding her body tight, trying to shield herself. Two more shots. Please God, don't let it be Thomas, she prayed. As she heard the sliding door begin to open, she held her breath and closed her eyes.

'Emily?' she heard Thomas's voice.

'Thomas ... Oh, Thomas.' She started to sob.

Thomas rushed over to her, gently lifting her off the floor and placing her on the couch. For a moment Emily just sat there, staring into space.

'It's OK, Emily. It's over,' Thomas said. 'It's done.'

Emily only nodded her head. She couldn't speak, her mind repeating the whizzing of the bullet over and over. Suddenly the front door crashed open and three police officers rushed in, their guns drawn. 'He's outside,' Thomas shouted. 'He's dead.'

Thomas called down to Annie and Martin and waited with Emily until they came. 'Thomas,' Annie said, 'are you all right?'

'I'm fine, but I have things I need to do. I want you and Martin to stay with Emily.'

'You go do what you have to,' Annie said as Thomas got up from the couch and headed for the veranda door. 'And Thomas ... thank you.'

'Emily,' Annie said, sitting down and covering Emily's still trembling hands with her own. 'You must have been terrified.'

'It happened so fast, Annie. I wasn't frightened until it was over. I was afraid he had killed Thomas.'

Martin brought both of them a brandy. His face was lined and ashen, and Emily noticed that his hand shook as he handed her the glass. 'That was much too close a call,' he said. 'A matter of minutes. If Thomas hadn't arrived when he did, I shudder—'

'Let's not talk about what ifs,' Annie said. 'Emily's safe and they've got him.'

One of the forensic team arrived. 'Sorry, Mr Maitland,' he said, pointing to one of the beautiful paintings that Emily had so admired. A small black hole surrounded by scorch marks pierced its center. 'We've got to—'

'Of course,' Martin said. 'We'll leave you to it.'

The three of them walked out and watched the scene unfolding just below. Sirens blared and flashing lights once again illuminated the night. There must have been six or seven police cars scattered across the lawns, and Emily could see Thomas directing the men. They swarmed this way and that, searching the bushes and collecting bits of evidence. There was a knock at the front door and Martin walked in to answer it.

At the entrance stood the medical examiner. Always sardonic, Van Trigt bowed his head slightly and said, 'Making a bit of a habit of this, are you, Mr Maitland?' Martin showed him to the veranda and he made his way to the scene. Emily could see the body lying there. She turned away and went inside.

Sarah and Jon arrived a few minutes later. Sarah ran first to her mother and then to Emily. 'I'm glad he's dead,' she said. 'At least it will save everyone from going through a trial.' You could hear the anger in her voice. Alex came in shortly after and sat with her father.

The few people who were still at the Bluffs soon started to make their way tentatively up the path towards Annie and Martin's. The sirens and flashing lights had become all too familiar and they were all worried about what had happened. Soon Christopher and Henri, Alice and Joe and Marietta and Nora were all seated around the living room. Martin told them what little he knew, but he couldn't answer their many questions.

'What have you decided to do about the Bluffs, Martin?' Marietta asked, her voice tremulous.

'We'll close for the month of January,' Martin answered. 'We've already started notifying people. Most have been pretty understanding. They've all read what's been going on down here. We're trying to set them up at other resorts.'

'We'll visit Alex in New York and Christopher in Paris. Take some time for ourselves. Have a real vacation,' Annie added.

Martin turned to Marietta. 'What we'll do after that, I don't—'

'We'll reopen,' Annie said. 'The Bluffs has been our life for over thirty years. I won't let him take that away from us.'

315

'Oh, thank God,' Marietta said. 'I don't know *what* I would have done. I mean, where *would* I go?'

It was a couple of hours before Thomas joined them. Emily could see the exhaustion on his face. 'Thomas, can you tell us anything?' Martin asked. 'Can you tell us *why*?'

Thomas spoke carefully. 'We don't know everything yet but it seems that Billy Dunlop was a low-level drug dealer who was trying to make his way up in that world. He obviously lured Ariana into a relationship. God knows how, but he was older, good looking, charming when he wanted to be and had an edge of excitement to him, I imagine. We believe he was trying to get her to carry a package, cocaine most likely, when she went to the States. She must have refused and he killed her.'

'For that?' Annie said. 'That bastard.'

'He couldn't trust that she wouldn't say anything. I'm afraid he believed Peggy saw him with Ariana. She hadn't, but she had seen him on the path and thought he seemed strange, out of place. Once he saw the sketch and heard there was a witness, he decided he had to get rid of her.'

'And Emily?' Sarah asked.

'The bracelet. He was afraid Emily would

remember how she lost her bracelet ... and she did. That's how we identified him. We were almost too late.'

'Do the others know?' Emily asked.

'They do. I called the Van Meeterens and Ted Lawson. They're relieved but I'm afraid this won't be over for them for a long time ... if ever.'

Thomas explained that he had to leave; there was much to do down at headquarters. They all thanked him for what he had done, but he seemed to take little comfort in that. He and Emily headed out to the veranda.

He held her close and whispered her name. 'What will you do, Emily? Will you leave tomorrow?'

'No, I'll wait till Friday.'

'Please, say you'll have dinner with me tomorrow night. We'll go somewhere quiet – somewhere where we can talk ... I'm so sorry things turned out like this. I'd hoped that we'd—'

'Hush, Thomas. It's not your fault. None of this is your fault. If it hadn't been for you...' But she didn't want to think about that. 'I'd love to have dinner tomorrow night. And Thomas, I thought that maybe, once this is all settled ... you could get some time off? I know New York is not the best in winter, but...'

'Oh, Emily, I'm sure I'd love New York in winter.' Thomas smiled.